BEAUTIFUL BLOOD

Lucius Shepard

SUBTERRANEAN PRESS 2014

First Edition

ISBN
978-1-59606-652-6

Subterranean Press
PO Box 190106
Burton, MI 48519

subterraneanpress.com

"BY NIGHT, THE CROOKED streets of Morningshade resounded with laughter, shrieks and contending musics, and were thronged with drunks, brawlers, vendors, whores, cutpurses, pickpockets and the precious few who were their targets—they pushed, jostled and shouldered their way along beneath a pall of smoke, a sluggish river of humanity dressed in rags and cheap gaud sloshing against the banks of taverns and gin shops, disreputable inns and bawdy houses, ramshackle buildings that leaned together like doddering grey-faced uncles with caved-in top hats made of tarpaper. And over it all, the vast bulge of piceous blackness that was Griaule's belly and side, from which depended a fringe of vines and clumped epiphytes, some dangling so low they nearly brushed the rooftops, showing in silhouette against the glowing blue darkness of the sky.

"As we pressed closer to the dragon, the crowds thinned, the cooking smells became less pervasive and the buildings grew less densely packed, until at last we came to the wide semi-circle of dirt (the site of a flea market by day) that bordered Griaule's bent foreleg and great taloned foot. Here there stood a single notable structure, a rickety construction made of weathered boards, replete with gables, bay window and other ornamental conceits—the Hotel Sin Salida, Morningshade's most infamous brothel. The hotel incorporated two of the talons into its foundation (they flanked the front door, forming a massive entranceway of age-yellowed bone) and rose an improbable nine stories, seeming on the verge of collapse, though it was actually quite stable, anchored by thick hawsers and cables to Griaule's scaly ankle, against which it was braced. With its spindly frame and treacherous outside staircases, it resembled a shabby, eccentric castle.

"Standing about on the steps were a half-dozen women with their breasts exposed, wearing satin trousers, and a larger number of unsavory-looking men, some carrying machetes. Scampering in and out amongst them, playing a game of tag, were a handful of children dressed in bright blue pants and blouses, a uniform that marked them as property of the hotel. They were initially oblivious to our approach, but as we came within earshot, they turned toward us, children and adults alike, displaying a disturbing unanimity of intense focus and neutral expression, as if responding to an inaudible signal—but then, almost instantly, they relaxed from this rigid posture and ran toward us, smiling and with open arms, inviting us to partake of the pleasures of the house."

Braulio DaSilva, *The House of Griaule*

1

T THE AGE OF twenty-six, Richard Rosacher, newly a medical doctor (he advertised the fact to no one, his diploma resting beneath a heap of soiled clothing on his bedroom floor), was possessed of a devout single-mindedness such as might have been attached to an educated man twice his age and of infinitely larger accomplishment. From earliest childhood he had been fascinated by the dragon Griaule, that mile-long beast paralyzed millennia before by a wizard's spell, beneath and about which the town of Teocinte had accumulated; and, as he approached his majority, that fascination was refined into an obsessive scientific curiosity. Running contrary to this virtue, however, was a wide streak of adolescent arrogance that left him prone to fits of temper. His rooms, occupying a portion of the second story of the Hotel Sin Salida in Morningshade (the poorest quarter of Teocinte, tucked so close beneath the dragon's side, it never knew the light of dawn), offended him not so much by their squalor, but by the poor relation in which they stood to the tastefully appointed surroundings in which he believed a person of his worth should be lodged. While he bore a genuine affection for many who quartered at the inn, rough sorts all (laborers, thieves, prostitutes, and the like), he believed himself destined for a loftier precinct, imagining that someday soon he would converse with poets, artists, fellow scientists, and cohabit with women whose beauty and grace were emblems of sensitive, carefully tended souls. This snobbish attitude was exacerbated by his outrage over the fact that the populace of Teocinte treated the dragon as an object of superstition, a godlike creature who manipulated their actions through exercise of its ancient will, and not as a biological freak, a gigantic lizard whose sole remarkable quality was as a treasure trove of scientific knowledge. Thus it was that when thwarted in his ambitions by Timothy Myrie, a disheveled shred of a man with no ambition of his own apart from that of drinking himself unconscious each and every night, Rosacher reacted along predictable lines.

The confrontation between the two men occurred late of an evening in Rosacher's sitting room, a narrow space with a sloping ceiling cut by pitch-coated roof beams, the plaster walls painted by the brush of time to a grayish cream, like egg gone off, and mapped by water stains the color of dried urine. Spider webs trellised the corners, belling in drafts that entered through a half-open bay window and, although the breeze carried a certain freshness (along with an undertone of sewage), it was unable to dispel the odor of innumerable sour lives. Rosacher had pushed sofa and chairs all to one end in order to accommodate an oak ice chest and a crudely carpentered workbench whereon rested scattered papers and a second-hand microscope; a cherrywood box containing vials, slides, and chemicals; a dirty dish bearing chicken bones and a crust of bread, the remnants of his supper; and an oil lamp that shed a feeble yellow light sufficient to point up the squalor of the place. Myrie, his pinched features shadowed by a slouch hat, clad in a greatcoat several sizes too large, stood by the bench, striking a pose that conveyed a casual disaffection, and Rosacher—his lean, handsome face, active eyes and glossy brown hair presenting by contrast an image of vitality—glared at him from an arms-length away. He wore a loose white shirt and moleskin knee-britches, and was holding out some crumpled banknotes to Myrie who, to his amazement, had rejected them.

"I need more," Myrie said. "I thought my heart would stop, I took such a fright."

"I can't afford more," Rosacher said firmly. "Next time, perhaps."

"Next time? I'll not be going back there soon. The things I saw…"

"Fine, then. That's fine. But we had a bargain."

"Too right we *had* a bargain. And now we're going to have a new bargain. I need a hundred more."

Rosacher's frustration plumed into anger. "It was a simple thing I asked. Any fool could have managed it!"

"If it's so simple, why not do it yourself?" Myrie cocked an ear, as if anticipating an answer. "I'll tell you why! 'Cause you don't much like the thought of crawling into the mouth of a fucking great dragon and drawing blood from his tongue! Not that I blame you. It's far from a pleasant experience." He stuck out his palm. "A hundred more's still on the cheap."

"Can't you get it through your head, man? I don't have it!"

"Then you're not having your precious blood, either." Myrie patted the breast of his coat. "Town's full of crazy folk these days, all wanting souvenirs. Chances are one of them will pay my price."

Fuming inwardly, Rosacher said, "All right! I'll get you the money."

Myrie smirked. "I thought you didn't have it."

"One of the girls downstairs will loan it to me."

"Got yourself a sweetheart, eh?" Myrie made an approving noise with his tongue. "Go on, then. Ask her!"

Rosacher fought back the urge to shout. "Will you at least put the blood in the ice chest? I don't wish it to degrade further."

Myrie cast a dubious look at the chest. "I reckon I'll keep it on my person until I see the hundred."

"For God's sake, man! She may be occupied. It may be some time before I can speak with her. Put the blood in the chest. I'll be back with the money as soon as I can."

"Which girl is it?"

"Ludie."

"The black bitch? Oh, she'll have it to spare. Very popular, she is." Myrie's tone waxed conspiratorial, as if he were imparting secret knowledge. "I'm told she's exceptional. Got a few extra muscles in her tra-la-la." He leered at Rosacher, as if anticipating confirmation of this fact.

"Please!" said Rosacher. "The blood."

Acting put upon, Myrie reached inside his coat and brought forth a veterinary syringe filled with golden fluid. He displayed it to Rosacher with an expression of exaggerated delight, as if showing a child a marvelous toy; then he opened the chest, set the syringe atop a block of ice, closed the lid and sat down upon it. "There now," he said. "It'll be safe 'til your return."

Rosacher stared at him with loathing, wheeled about and made for his bedroom.

"Here! Where you going?" Myrie called.

"To fetch my boots!"

Rosacher proceeded into the bedroom and snatched his boots from beneath the bed. It galled him to beg money of Ludie. As he struggled to pull the left boot on, the disarray of his life, patched stockings, a raveled vest, a shabby cloak, all his ill-used possessions seemed to be commenting on the paucity of his existence. A flood of cold resolve snuffed out his sense of humiliation. That he should allow the likes of Myrie to practice extortion! That he should be delayed an instant in beginning his study of the blood! It was intolerable. He flung down the boots and strode back into the sitting room, each step reinvigorating his anger. Myrie shot him a quizzical glance and appeared on the verge of speaking, but before he could utter a word Rosacher seized him by the collar, yanked him upright and slung him headfirst into the wall. The little man crumpled, giving forth a sodden sound. Once again Rosacher grabbed his collar and this time slammed his face into the floorboards. Spitting curses, he rolled Myrie onto his back, lifted him to his feet and threw him against the door. He barred an arm beneath his chin, pinning him there while he groped for the door knob. Blood from his nose filmed over Myrie's mouth. A pink bubble swelled between his lips and popped. Rosacher wrenched open the door and shoved him out into the corridor, where he collapsed. He intended to hurl a final curse, but he trembled with rage and his thoughts would not cohere. He stood watching Myrie struggle to his hands and knees, deriving a primitive satisfaction from the sight, yet at the same time dismayed by his loss of control. Merited, he told himself, though it had been. Unable to develop an appropriate insult, he kicked Myrie's hat after him and closed the door.

2

HEMATOLOGY HAD BEEN ROSACHER'S speciality in medical school, but the poetic character of blood, that red whisper of life twisting through caverns in the flesh, had intrigued him long before he entered university. And so it was a natural evolution that his scholarly concerns conjoin with his fascination regarding the dragon to create an obsession with Griaule's blood. It astonished him that no one else had thought to study it. Blood pumped by a heart that beat once every thousand years, never congealing, maintaining its liquidity against inexorable physical logic...the potential benefits arising from such a study were unimaginable. Yet now, peering at the slide he had made, what he saw bore so marginal a relation to human blood, he wondered whether a study would prove rewarding. To begin with, the blood had no recognizable cells. It abounded with microscopic structures, darkly figured against the golden plasma, but these structures multiplied and changed in shape and character, rapidly passing through a succession of changes prior to vanishing—after more than an hour of observation, Rosacher had begun to believe that Griaule's blood was a medium that contained every possible shape, each one busy changing into every other. He grew fatigued, but rubbed his eyes and splashed water onto his face and kept on peering through the microscope, hoping a dominant pattern would emerge. When none did he was tempted to accept that the blood was magical stuff, impervious to informed scrutiny; yet he was unwilling to let go of obsession, seduced by the infinity of pattern disclosed by the slide, the mutable contours of the mysterious structures, the shifting mosaic of gold and shadowy detail, pulsing as if they reflected the process of an embedded rhythmic force, as if the blood were its own engine and required no heartbeat to sustain its vitality. And such might be the case. No other explanation suited. The matter at issue, then, would be to illuminate the workings of this engine, to discover if its function could be replicated in human blood. He considered going for a walk. Physical activity would allow his excited thoughts to settle and he might then be able to construct an empirical strategy; but he could not pull himself away from the microscope, captivated by the protean beauty of the design unfolding before him, one moment having the smudged delicacy of a rubbing and the next becoming sharply etched against the golden background.

It was apparent that Griaule's blood contained an agent that was proof against degradation, against the processes of time. Whether this was due to its intrinsic nature or to the enchantment that had rendered the dragon immobile, Rosacher could not speculate; but it occurred to him that the mutable constituency of the blood, the evolution of its patterns, might reflect an ongoing adjustment to the flow of time through matter, an adjustment that prevented it from decaying. This insight seemed not to arise from a process of deduction but from the blood itself, to be basic information carried by its patterns, information that he had absorbed by observing its changes—though to accept such an outrageous proposition was not in his character, Rosacher found he could not reject it. With acceptance came the recognition that the blood might offer not merely an anti-clotting agent, but a remedy to the depre-dations of time itself and thus to every ill associated with aging. So entranced was he by the flickering mosaic on the slide, he scarcely registered Ludie's knock.

"Richard?" she called. "Are you there?"

Impatiently, he threw open the door. She wore a petti-coat and a frilled bodice, and her kittenish, cocoa-colored face was troubled. He was about to tell her to come back later, when she was pushed aside by a gaunt lantern-jawed man. He towered over Myrie, who peeked from behind him, and was dressed in much the same manner: great-coat, mud-caked boots, and a slouch hat. His acromegalic features were split by a grotesque smile, brown teeth leaning at rustic angles in the inflamed gums.

"Hello!" he said cheerfully, and clubbed Rosacher in the temple with his fist.

When Rosacher had regained sufficient of his senses to be aware of his surroundings, he discovered that he was trussed hand and foot, and lying on the floor. Ludie huddled beside him and two men—Myrie and the man who had struck him—were ransacking the room, tossing papers and books about, emptying shelves, knocking over his microscope. This abuse caused Rosacher to complain feebly, attracting the notice of the big man. He dropped to a knee beside Rosacher, grabbed him by the shirtfront and lifted him so their noses were inches apart. To Rosacher, dazed, his skull throbbing, that leathery face was an abstract of mottling, moles, and crevices, dominated by two mismatched eyes, one brown, one green—a barren terrain in which two oddly discolored puddles had formed.

"Where's your money?" the man asked, his rotten breath gushing forth, as from the sudden opening of a stable door.

Rosacher had no thought of lying—he indicated his jacket, which lay across the back of a chair, and watched with muddled despair as the man rifled his wallet. Beside him, Ludie made an affrighted noise.

"This can't be all!" The big man thrust the few bills he had extracted from the wallet at Rosacher. "It won't do! Not by half!"

Myrie appeared at his shoulder. "I told you he'd no money, Arthur. It's his possessions what are valuable."

"His possessions? This sorry lot?" The big man pushed him away in disgust and, as Myrie fought to maintain his balance, Rosacher thought how strangely genteel a fate it was to be robbed and beaten by two men named Timothy and Arthur.

Myrie, who had fetched up against the workbench, hefted the microscope. "This here's bound to bring a price!"

Arthur stared at it. "What's it for?"

"He uses it to look at blood."

"Blood, you say?"

"It lets him look at it close-like."

"Oh, well. Now that is a treasure!"

Myrie beamed.

"Yes, indeed," Arthur went on. "Why we'll just carry this little item over to Ted Crandall's shop. Ted, I'll say, I know you've dozens...No, hundreds of people begging for a device that'll let them look at blood. Close-like!" He gave a forlorn shake of his head. "God help me, Tim. You're a fucking champion!"

Myrie's smile drooped; then he brightened and went to the ice chest. "There's this!" he said, producing the syringe. "He sets great store by it."

Arthur examined the syringe under the lamp. "This is the blood?"

"I reckon someone might pay dear for it," Myrie said, and gestured toward Rosacher.

Arthur gazed in disgust at Myrie; without a word, he thumbed the plunger and squirted golden blood onto the little man's coat. Myrie yelped and flung himself away.

"You brainless ass!" Arthur said, squirting him again. "Dragging me from the tavern for this! I'm marking tonight down. You owe me plenty for this exercise." He appeared to be on the verge of leaving, but then caught Rosacher's eye. "What are you looking at?"

Rosacher, not yet up to speaking clearly, managed a perhaps intelligible denial of looking.

"I understand." Arthur flourished the syringe, which still contained a small amount of the golden fluid. "You're concerned about the blood."

"I..." Rosacher hawked up mucus from his throat. "I wish you'd put it back."

Arthur cupped his ear. "You wish what? I didn't catch the last bit."

"The blood will degrade if it's left out in the air."

"Too right! We wouldn't want it to degrade. I'll put it somewhere safe, shall I?"

Arthur dropped to one knee and gripped him by the throat. An instant later the syringe bit into Rosacher's left thigh. He cried out and tried to shake free, but

Myrie kneeled and pinned his legs as Arthur pushed in the plunger.

The only immediate effect of the injection that Rosacher could discern was a sensation of cold that spread through the muscles of his thigh. Grinning broadly, Arthur dropped the half-empty syringe on his chest and stood.

"Well, now," he said. "I believe my work here is done."

He strode to the door and Myrie, after seizing the opportunity to spit in Rosacher's face, hurried after him.

Ludie came to her knees and began working at his bonds, saying, "They forced me, Richard! I'm sorry!"

She continued to talk, prying at the knots, freeing his arms, his legs, asking if he was all right, her speech muffled as though she were speaking from inside a closet. The numbing cold that had followed the bite of the syringe dissipated and warmth flooded Rosacher's body, attended by a feeling of glorious well-being. He thought he should sit up, but the impulse did not rise to the level of will. Everything in sight had acquired a luster. Spiderwebs glistened like strands of polished platinum; the boards gleamed with the grainy perfection of gray marble; his broken glassware glittered with prismatic glory, a scatter of rare gems; his possessions scattered across the floor seemed part of a decorative scheme, as if the apartment's sorry condition were the work of an artist who, guided by a decadent sensibility, had sought to counterfeit shabbiness by using the richest of materials. Ordinarily he thought of Ludie as a lovely girl, but now she struck him as the acme of feminine beauty. Her hair, kept short like a skullcap, gave an elfin look to the clever, triangular face with its sharp cheekbones and large eyes and lips that, due to a slight malocclusion, lapsed naturally into a sulky expression. The hollow at the base of her throat that each morning she sweetened with lime and honey water; her breasts barely constrained by the lacy shells of her bodice...His cataloguing of her physical charms grew more intimate and, energized by arousal, he stood and swept her up and carried her to his bed. Startled by his sudden recovery, she asked what he was doing. He sought to respond, but his thoughts effloresced rather than developing in a linear progression, evolving into elusive, inexpressible logics and fantasies. Touching her skin was like touching warm silk and all the opulent particulars of her body seemed an architecture created to house a central bloom of light. Her anima, he thought. Her spirit. As he joined with her, their flesh glued together in an animal rhythm, he sought that light, plunging toward it, wedding his light to hers in a spectacular union that concluded with a shattering of prisms behind his eyes and a confusing multiplicity of pleasurable sensations that he did not believe were entirely his own.

At long last, leaving her drowsing, Rosacher threw on his trousers, went to the sitting room window and stood gazing out over the rooftops of adjoining shanties and the grander, slightly less ruinous buildings that spread in crooked rows up along the slope of a hill that merged with Griaule's side. Of the dragon he could see only a great mound of darkness limned by the glow of the newly risen moon. The buildings were picked out here and there by flickering lights, and these lights appeared knitted together by golden lines that formed a constellate shape. Not the predictable shape of a bull or a warrior or a throne, but a complicated mapping of lines and points like an illuminated blueprint. He began to suspect that the pattern they made, like the patterns in Griaule's blood, contained information that was imprinting itself upon the electrical patterns of his brain, translating its essentials into a comprehensible form. After staring at it for a quarter of an hour he realized that he had the solution to his problems in hand.

It was such a simple answer that he was tempted to reject it on the grounds of simplicity, assuming that a solution so obvious must have flaws—but his only question was whether or not a small dose would produce the same effects created by the massive dose he had absorbed. When he could detect none other, he addressed the ethical considerations. Setting the plan in motion would be an abrogation of his medical oath, malfeasance of the highest order...yet was adherence to an oath more ethically persuasive than funding his research? Toward dawn, the effects of the dragon's blood ebbing, Rosacher experienced irritability, a symptom such as might attach to a withdrawal; yet this soon vanished, though his feeling of contentment and well-being remained. He wondered if whether the irritability might be due to the size of the dose with which he had been injected. If the blood were not physically addictive, that might be an impediment to his plan. But then he realized that a psychological addiction would be more than sufficient for the purposes. The populace of Morningshade, powerless and possessed of no legitimate prospects, would pay dearly to see their hovels transformed into palaces, their lovers into sexual ideals, and they had no will—none he had noticed, at any rate—to resist temptation, whatever toll it might extract.

3

T HE TOWN OF TEOCINTE spread from the dragon's
side to sprawl across a substantial portion of the
Carbonales Valley, flowing over a lumpy hill
(known as Haver's Roost, referring to an inn once situated
there) that bulged up from the valley floor, atop which
stood the white buildings of government and a church
under construction—from this point continued to spread
in all directions for a mile and more, giving out into clus-
ters of ramshackle structures no less derelict than those of
Morningshade; yet while Griaule's paralysis was a condition of apparent permanence, no one had yet chosen to
build upon the ground close by his head, doubtless unsettled by the prospect of walking out their door and seeing
the dragon's gaping mouth the first thing each morning.

Thus the area remained overgrown by stands of palmettos interspersed with shrimp plants and wild hibiscus, acacias, banana and thorn trees.

Standing amid the brush at dusk three days after the encounter with Myree and Arthur, Rosacher came to appreciate that Myree might have underestimated the worth of his labors. Viewed from a hundred feet away, Griaule's head, lowered to the ground, towered above all, looking in its grotesque conformation to be the fantastic conceit of a master builder, an improbable construction that transformed the entrance to a palace into an immense bestial image. The golden scales below the sagittal crest gleamed dully, holding the last of the sun, and one eye, visible beneath the bulge of the orbital ridge, showed black, as if the socket were empty. Framed by the upraised snout and twisted fangs, each as tall as a sabal palm and so festooned with moss that they had the appearance of scrimshaw, the cavern of Griaule's throat might have been a gateway into the nether regions.

It was cold, as cold as ever it got in the valley, and Rosacher's breath steamed. As the light faded he began to hear noises issuing from the mouth, perhaps from even deeper within the dragon's body, belonging to the creatures that wintered there: the ululations of frogs, bats shrilling, and hoarse, strangely exultant cries that he was unable to identify. The shadows merged into true night and insects announced its onset with a whining sizzle. His mind ached with fear, yet he forced himself to move toward Griaule, having to throw his legs forward, his pack bumping against his shoulders like a second, slower heart.

Drawing near the mouth, he removed a lantern from the pack and lit the wick with a trembling hand. The scales of the underjaw, no more than six feet distant, glinted among tall weeds. He raised the lantern, illuminating a section of jaw some thirty feet above; higher yet, a portion of gum, brown as tobacco juice, came to light, as did the base of a fang. The wind blew across Griaule's face and a breath of dry, dusty coolness briefly dominated the vegetable odors. Rosacher hooked the lantern to his pack, buttressed his mind against panic, and climbed, using vines hanging from the lip like strings of leathery drool to haul himself along. Minutes later, he slung a leg over the lip. He scrambled to his feet in a panic, turning this way and that, holding up the lantern to reveal stunted, pale-leaved shrubs sprouting from soil that had accumulated over the centuries; the head-high thickness of the tongue, a mounded shape shrouded in ground moss, and the dim concavity of the dragon's cheek. Night sounds closed in around him—bleeps, rustlings, and what might have been thin screams—but he could detect no movement. Calmer now, he pushed through a fringe of vegetation to the tongue and suspended the lantern off the end a branch. From the pack he removed a veterinary syringe, the same Myrie had used. Cautiously, he plucked at the moss until he had cleared a circular area. The tongue was dead black. He placed the tip of the needle against it, but over a minute passed before he mustered the courage to shove it home, applying all his weight in order to penetrate the surface. He waited for a cthonic reaction, a great shudder or grumble of complaint. None occurred, but his anxiety did not subside until he had withdrawn the needle and emptied its contents into a flask. He repeated the process twice more, coming to scoff at Myrie's fright and his own. There was nothing to harm him here. Only bugs, bats, and lizards. He worked hastily, but not too hastily for the sake of efficiency, filling twenty flasks, nearly a gallon of blood, and nesting them in cotton padding. In the future, he thought, he would contract this work not to men such as Myrie, but to the citizens of Hangtown, the village surmounting the dragon's back where lived an assortment of outcasts. Though eccentric to a fault, they were honest enough and their familiarity with Griaule would preclude any repetition of the scene he had enacted with Myrie. He would need more blood, of that he was certain. Synthesizing a drug from a fluid whose constituency was a complete mystery would likely remain beyond the scope of his capabilities. Perhaps he could resolve that mystery with time and work, but his initial task was to determine an effective dosage and to find a suitable medium that would allow the drug to be absorbed into the bloodstream (syringes being in short supply).

A thin silver crescent sailed clear above the hills, appearing to hover beside a fang partially cast in silhouette by its light. To Rosacher, shouldering his pack, the sight had the unreal vividness of an opium dream—it appeared to infect the rest of the landscape, lending an occult accent to the dark sky with its freckling of stars and the brush-covered field and the flickering orange lamps in the windows of outlying shanties on the hillside, like an illustration in a book of exotic fairy tales. Odd, he thought, that he could be reflective after having been terrified not long before. It was a transformation like that he had experienced in the narcotic grip of the blood, and he wondered if it were still in his system... or perhaps what he felt was not a relaxation from fear, but Griaule's approval. The citizens of Morningshade would suggest that since Rosacher had been allowed to draw blood, he must be obeying Griaule's will, and that his calmness was a sign the dragon had given its blessing to the act. Because they believed that through the exertion of his will Griaule controlled every facet of their lives, they might further suggest that the similarity of effect between this blessing of calm and that of the injected blood proved he had been Griaule's pawn from the beginning. They might have told him that, if the dragon had been angry, the blood would have changed to acid in his flesh. He was not inclined to ridicule such notions as once he might, but the truth of the matter was irrelevant. Whether or not as a result of the dragon's manipulation, he was embarked upon a course from which it would be difficult to turn aside.

He moved toward a corner of the mouth, hoping to locate a less precipitous path of descent, and heard sibilance, like a chorus of whispers. He stopped dead in his tracks and the chorus subsided. A fierce tension stiffened his muscles. He lifted the lantern, but saw nothing inimical. Yet when he went forward again, after a half-dozen steps the whispering sounded again, louder and somehow larger, as if the number of whisperers had doubled or tripled. The voices held a querulous note, a charge of mean-spirited intensity, and he did not try to find their source, but picked up his pace, hurrying through the shrubs, skirting a forking of the tongue, head down, his fear restored in full. The voices fell silent, but as he approached the spot where he intended to begin his descent, they started up a third time, so shrill that he could no longer think of them as whisperings, but rather as an insane singing—they had a papery quality reminiscent of the scraping of cicadas. Tremulously, he held the lantern high over his head. Massed together, covering the illuminated portion of the interior cheek wall, were a host of insects. Large insects, each about the size of a two-year-old child, they resembled crickets with gray chitinous bodies, their many-faceted eyes pointed with reflected lantern light. Judging by the volume of their singing, by the way they stirred, seething forward, as if part of a tide, Rosacher guessed there were thousands more hidden by the dark, an army covering the upper wall and palette. They appeared to be one creature with a single cruel, inscrutable face replicated over and over; their feelers waved and their legs worked slightly, causing the tide of bodies to appear to billow and dimple like a mat bearing a repetitive design floating on the surface of choppy water. His astonishment gave way to terror. His bones were stalks of ice, his muscles incompliant. He tottered closer to the lip. The singing broke off and the insects surged lower on the cheek wall. Rosacher stopped walking and the singing resumed. He could, he thought, hurl himself off the lip and hope to snag a vine, or that the bushes below would break his fall. He tried to slow his breathing, to gather himself, certain that the insects would swarm toward him; but instead of attacking, their voices again fell silent and they swung about, all in unison, so they were every one of them facing toward the depths of the dragon's throat.

Their synchronous action disconcerted Rosacher nearly as much as an attack would have done. He imagined a controlling agency that might pose a more significant threat than that of the insects themselves, and he was half-persuaded to accept the view that Griaule was not simply a moribund lizard of Brobdingnagian proportions, but a fabulous presence whose potentials were myriad and in large part unknown. He resisted the impulse to discover what had commanded the insects' attention, afraid of looking away from them, but after a second or two, he turned to the throat. At first he saw only darkness, but then he noticed movement, though not the sort of movement he might have expected. A clot of atramentous black had materialized from the lesser blackness and billowed toward him, as if it were an entity that possessed the qualities of a gaseous cloud, one evolving into a shape and acquiring solidity, growing increasingly compact and menacing in form. A lion, he thought. No, a bull...or a crocodile with aspects of both bull and lion. He backed away from the cloud and, as it closed the space between them with a sudden surge, developing into a towering column that trembled with energy, on the verge—he believed—of assuming some final, dreadful shape, fear overwhelmed him and he flung himself from the dragon's lip and fell screaming into the brush below.

4

ROSACHER'S SECOND THOUGHT ON waking the next morning was that someone must have happened upon him lying unconscious in the brush and carried him to their home and there tended to his injuries; yet he could not think of one of his acquaintance with access to such a splendid bedchamber. The ceiling was high and cream-colored, worked with designs of leaves and roses and other flowers from which cunning, childlike faces emerged (his initial presumption had been that he was the prisoner of malefic spirits). Paintings in gilt frames hung on the walls and all the furnishings—chairs, bureau, cabinets—were exquisitely carved and finished. He swung his legs off the side of the bed (wide enough for four; green silk sheets and a golden coverlet; pineapple posts of teak with ivory inlays) and was astounded to discover that he had no aches and pains whatsoever. Either he had been lucky in the extreme or else he had been unconscious for several days, sufficiently long for his scrapes and bruises to mend. He crossed to a window, flung open the drapes, and realized that he must be in one of the mansions that occupied the slopes of Haver's Roost. Looking eastward across the sun-drenched town, he could make out the low, patchwork roofs of Morningshade a half-mile away and the dragon's ribcage rising above them, its back mapped by dense thickets and a wood, the rude shanties of Hangtown shadowed by the sagittal crest. The view seemed familiar, yet he could have sworn he had never been at that window before. He wandered about the room, touching picture frames, a rosewood end table, the gold and green rug that simulated a pattern of dragon scales, a leather-covered jewelry box holding cufflinks and coins and a dozen things more, and each object he touched brought to mind a memory, a fleeting association baffling in its familiarity. He stopped in front of a mirror. His hair was no longer a mass of dark curls; it was trimmed to stubble. He wore a gold earring bearing a green gemstone. Touching it, he knew it had been a gift from Ludie. Above his right eye, a scar whitened a portion of his eyebrow, an injury received in his fall from the dragon's lip four years ago...

This revelation, if revelation it were, if he were not lying unconscious beneath Griaule's lip and having a dream, rooted him to the spot. He examined the memory, attempting to decide whether it had the heft of the actual, but other memories lurched into his mind, shoving one another aside in their haste to make themselves known, filling his brain to bursting with a flood of trivia (appointments to be kept. problems to be dealt with and so on), from which he distilled the undeniable fact that his plan had worked. He was wealthy. This was *his* house. Each and every day his factories produced a sufficient quantity of the drug in smoke-able form to supply the addicts of Teocinte and Port Chantay, and he planned to branch out, to export the drug to other towns and develop a pastille that would allow the drug to dissolve in the mouth, suitable for those who did not smoke. Dizzy with this influx of memory, Rosacher dropped into an easy chair and sought a star by which to steer through the sea of information. How was it possible that he could have these memories and yet never have experienced their reality? Was he to believe that he had been operating in a somnambulistic state for four years? There were cases in which a blow to the head caused a temporary condition similar to the one he seemed to have suffered, but in none of them had the patient prospered while enduring that condition. Four years! His memories relating to that time had little flavor or substance. It was as if he lived those years and yet had not lived them, as if he had riffled through the pages of that portion of his life, skipping ahead in his book of days to this particular day and hour. The memories were scraps, pieces of a jigsaw puzzle—fitted together, they assembled a visual image and embodied a related comprehension in each of which a digest history resided...and yet they transmitted almost nothing of the emotional context.

The bedchamber door opened and Ludie walked in, a sheaf of papers in hand. She wore riding breeches, boots, and a loose linen shirt, belted at the waist, and looked scarcely a day older than he recalled, still lovely—but a mask of hard neutrality tempered her beauty. That look, the attitude it embodied, cued another trickle of memories. They had once been monogamous, but as he involved himself more deeply in business, they had drifted apart and now he had his women and she her horses, her daylong trips into the valley where she would rendezvous with lovers, men and women both, and Rosacher's relationship with her had become a convenience, held together by a shred of reflex intimacy that disguised their fundamental indifference to one another—they were partners (Ludie had helped finance the early stages of the business) and they trusted each other in that way, but trust no longer extended into the emotional realm. Rosacher felt himself slipping into a suit of reactions that accommodated this state of affairs, yet he also regretted that things had reached this pass and struggled to sustain a nostalgic view of her.

She held out the papers to him. "Arthur's downstairs."

Rosacher continued to stare.

"It's the figures you asked for," she said. "The estimate of next year's earnings. And the notes for the rest of your presentation." When he did not take them, she shook the papers at him. "You should look these over before you leave."

"What are you up to today?" he asked.

A flicker of displeasure—she tossed the papers onto an easy chair. "I'm going for a ride."

"I'd like to see you this evening."

"*See* me?"

"Spend some time with you."

"I don't..."

"I hoped we might dine together."

She folded her arms. "Why? What do you want?"

"Not much. A few hours of your company."

She started to speak, hesitated, and said stiffly, "If you've a problem with the way I've been handling the books, I want to hear it now."

"I want to see you. Can that be so difficult to comprehend? My God! How long has it been since we spent an evening together?"

"I haven't kept track."

"Nor I...but it must be months."

She shrugged. "If you say so." Then, after a pause: "Very well. I'll cancel my plans."

That comment touched off yet another rush of confusing memories, these relating to his presentation, and Rosacher experienced a flash of unease—there were so many details to sort through. "Perhaps I should post-pone the presentation. We have a lot to talk about."

"Are you mad? We've been working toward this for nearly five years. Don't worry. They may have sum-moned you to receive their reprimand, but you'll have them scrambling to see which one of them can be your best friend before the hour's out."

She said this last harshly, as if it were an indictment, and then went to a closet, selected a white suit and laid it out on the bed. She adopted a thoughtful pose. "Perhaps your green shirt. It'll strike a flamboyant note. That's the image you want to present. Those stodgy old men will see you dressed like a parrot, dismissive of their conservative conventions, and they'll admire you for it. They'll disapprove of you at first, of course. But they'll come to recognize that you're establishing your inde-pendence from them. They'll view your disrespect as the byproduct of a bold personal style, and they'll respect that in you…so long as you make it worth their while."

She had grown angry as she spoke or, better said, she had let slip her stoic mask and shown him her normal level of resentment.

"Ludie," he said helplessly.

"I'll be in my quarters at eight o'clock," she said, going to the door. "Try to be punctual."

After she had gone he wondered if it was possible to restore the relationship. The council summons pressed in on him—he recalled its importance and his mind swarmed with details. He selected a green silk shirt from the closet and laid it beside the suit in order to gauge the effect, concluding that Ludie had been accurate in her judgment. It struck precisely the right note.

ARTHUR HONEYMAN, THE gaunt giant who had broken into Rosacher's apartment and assaulted him, had changed his outward aspect to a far greater degree than had Rosacher, though Arthur's transformation was by way of a refinement. Honeyman dressed well these days, given to collarless shirts and embroidered satin jackets that lent him a dandified air ill-suited to his rough-hewn features and bony frame. He smiled incessantly in order to show off his false teeth. They were not white but, thanks to jade inlays, were decorated so as to resemble moss-covered rocks—when he opened his mouth, they gave the impression that you were looking into a forbidding cavern. On the day he had hired Arthur, sitting at the desk in his office, a room adjoining his old apartments, Rosacher made new teeth a condition of his employment.

"The health of your body and that of your teeth are not separate issues," Rosacher told him. "If you don't take care of them, sooner or later they're bound to cause a serious infection and you'll be of no use to me. Then there's the consideration of your appearance. I want you to frighten people, but I don't think it's necessary to make them giddy with fear."

"Will it hurt?" Arthur asked.

"Yes. I can do the extractions painlessly, but there'll be some bruising of the tissues. However, you'll suffer more living with a mouth like that than you will in losing the teeth."

Arthur shuffled his feet, glanced out the window. "Why're you doing this? After what I done to you, it don't make sense."

"Everyone in Morningside is afraid of you," said Rosacher. "I've been observing you for several months and you're not unintelligent, though your methods of intimidation are unnecessarily crude. Most importantly, you're not an addict."

"Too right! I'd sooner take poison than smoke a pipe of mab (this the name the citizens of Morningshade applied to the drug, being an acronym for 'more and better'). I don't need my view of the world tarted up. I prefer to see things as they are."

"An admirable trait," said Rosacher. "One I've grown to appreciate." He got to his feet and came around the desk to stand in front of Arthur. "The past is the past. There's no need to dwell on it. I can help you and you can help me by dealing with problems that may arise. What I'm proposing is a business relationship pure and simple." He held out his hand. "Do we have an accord?"

"I'm your man!" Arthur shook his hand gingerly, as if taking pains not to injure him anew. "I'll deal with your problems. You can trust to that."

Rosacher was not inclined to extend his trust. For all his coarse exterior, Arthur was no fool and, sooner or later, the instincts bred by his rough-and-tumble existence would turn his intellect in a treacherous direction. Rosacher believed, however, he could find ways to keep him occupied.

Three and a half years later, armed with teeth that were no longer new, grinning fiercely at every passerby, his huge frame draped in a jacket of cherry-colored satin embroidered in white silk, hair held back from his shoulders by a gay matching ribbon, Arthur accompanied Rosacher to the top of Haver's Roost. People cleared out of the giant's path, falling back to either side of the winding street; others came to the windows and doorways of the mansions of brick and undressed stone that lined it, made curious by the passage of this two-man parade. At the summit of the hill lay a cobbled square ringed by buildings of pinkish stucco with ironwork balconies and red tile roofs, open on one end (the opening was due to be closed off by a cathedral, its foundations already laid and a single wall erected). It was toward the largest building, a three-story affair with ornamental iron bars over the windows, that they proceeded.

"I've never been up here before." Arthur sniffed the air. "Don't smell near as ripe as Morningshade."

Rosacher mounted the steps. "I think you'll find the stench more familiar once we're inside."

A slender, dark-haired man, appearing to be four or five years younger than Rosacher, sat on a bench in the mahogany-paneled vestibule on the second floor, outside the council chamber, clutching a leather artist's portfolio, listening as a functionary explained that he would have to wait until Mr. Rosacher finished his business before the council. On hearing this, the young man jumped up and demanded an immediate audience. Rosacher stepped in and said, "Excuse me. Mister...?"

"Cattanay," said the man, giving the name an angry emphasis, pronouncing each syllable with biting precision. "Meric Cattanay."

"Richard Rosacher. You have a proposal to put before the council?"

"I've been here since yesterday. I've come all the way from..."

"Believe me, Mister Cattanay. I understand your frustration. But I think I can assure you that the council will be in a more receptive mood after I have done than they are at the moment."

Somewhat mollified, yet still agitated, Cattanay expressed doubt as to Rosacher's claim, but when Rosacher told him that his business involved a considerable financial settlement, he sat down again. And when Rosacher inquired what his proposal entailed, he opened his portfolio and displayed a number of sketches that detailed a scheme for killing Griaule by means of poisoned paint applied to his skin. The idea seemed ludicrous on the face of it, yet Rosacher was forced to acknowledge that the basic notion was ingenious. He asked how long it might take to complete the job.

"I'm not sure," said Cattanay. "It will take two years at least to organize the project, to build the scaffolding and vats in which to mix the paint. We'll have to employ dozens of men, perhaps a hundred and more, to supply us with timber for fuel. That'll require another year or two. Then we'll have to create the painting and give the poison time to act. The whole process could take twenty or thirty years. Maybe more. I imagine something will go wrong every single day…problems I haven't envisioned."

Arthur snorted in derision and Cattanay glared at him. "They've run through all the unsubtle methods of killing him and failed," he said. "You know, burning him, stabbing him, and so forth. Of course now I think about it there's one method they haven't essayed. They could hold up a gigantic portrait of this fellow to Griaule's face"—he jabbed his thumb at Arthur—"and make a loud noise. I expect that might do the job."

Arthur snarled and reached for the knife tucked into his waistband, but Rosacher put a hand on his forearm by way of restraint and said to Cattanay, "Fascinating! How did you come up with the idea?"

"Some friends and I were in a tavern and we got to talking about schemes to make money. Painting the dragon was one of the schemes. I've fleshed it quite a bit since that evening, but the original idea, it was a joke, really. A joke made by a group of friends who'd had too much to drink."

The functionary, who had vanished into the council chamber while Cattanay described his scheme, returned and told Rosacher that he could go in.

Inside the chamber, an austere, spacious room with thick beams supporting the ceiling and windows overlooking the valley, offering a view of the hills enclosing its eastern reach, five men sat in high-backed chairs at a mahogany table, a ceramic pitcher and glasses set before them. With a single exception, they were fleshy and gray-haired, clad in sober suits, but the bearded man at their center, Wallace Febres-Cordero, possessed a gravitas the others did not and, though Rosacher had not met him until that moment, he divined from this brief observance that Febres-Cordero was the person he would have to sway. He took a seat in a wooden chair (the only one available) facing the table and Arthur stationed himself at his shoulder.

"Good morning, gentlemen," Rosacher said. "I'm Richard Rosacher and this is my associate, Arthur Honeyman. How can we assist you?"

"As you know," said Febres-Cordero in a mannered baritone, "the council has no authority over you as regards the production of drugs. We have no laws that would apply, yet we may find ourselves obligated to write new law should you continue on your present course."

"And why is that?" Rosacher asked.

LUCIUS SHEPARD

"My God, man!" A thin, balding council member at the end of the table, Paltz by name, brought the flat of his hand down with a smack. "You've addicted half the population of Morningshade to your poison!"

"It's closer to three-quarters, but let's not quibble," said Rosacher.

"We've had numerous complaints about your activities," said Febres-Cordero. "Every moral authority is up in arms against you."

"To whom are you referring?"

"The Church, for one."

"The Church as moral authority." Rosacher chuckled. "Now there's a fresh idea."

The florid face of the heavyset man sitting on Febres-Cordero's left, Councilman Rooney, grew purplish and he said, "You come here dressed like a popinjay and attempt to..."

"I think we should give Mister Rosacher the opportunity to defend himself." Febres-Cordero glanced along the table and then looked to Rosacher.

"Indeed, I would welcome the opportunity to speak," said Rosacher. "Though not to defend myself, but instead to offer an alternative course of action. Have any of you gentlemen smoked mab?"

"Now you're being impertinent," Febres-Cordero said. "I warn you, do not try our patience."

"I intended no impertinence. I merely wished to know whether or not you were conversant with the drug."

"We have interviewed a number of addicts and understand its effects."

"Did any of these addicts strike you as derelicts? Were they pale and sickly as with opium addicts, or were they hale and neatly attired? Did they not earn an honorable wage?"

Councilman Savedra, a vulturous, stoop-shouldered man, older than the rest, said, "If the thrust of your argument is to be that the drug causes no physical harm to the addict, it does not touch upon the moral issues."

"It is an element of my argument, but not its sole thrust. And it's not the health of the individual that concerns me so much as the health of the community." Rosacher stood and went a few paces along the table. "Should the council rule against me in this, I will happily move my business to Port Chantay or another of the coastal towns. It will be an inconvenience, nothing more. But before you banish me, I beg you to let me speak without interruption so I can present my thoughts in a coherent fashion."

"You asked a question," said Savedra. "I answered. You may proceed."

"Rhetorical questions require no answer, but never mind. I thank the councilman for his comment, because it brings me round to my next point." Rosacher moved to a window and gazed out across the valley. "Teocinte is poor. Of all the valley towns, it has—or had—the highest incidence of crime. Morningshade is its least prosperous and most dangerous quarter. The economy of the town is based upon agrarian concerns and a handful of mining operations. These provide an excellent life for a small minority, but the people of Morningshade and the various outlying communities do not fully participate in that economy. Until recently, they have subsisted chiefly by means of preying upon the wealthy and upon one another. Over the past four years, however, the incidence of crime has steadily dropped in Morningshade. When I dwelled there we only saw the constabulary when a crime had been perpetrated against the wealthy. Now, I'm told, they're scarcely seen at all. There has been a precipitous drop in crime and this is directly attributable to use of mab. I have hundreds…"

"Balderdash!" said Rooney.

"I have hundred of addicts in my employ," said Rosacher, ignoring him. "And I expect to employ hundreds more during the next twelve months alone. They none of them exhibit the violent and erratic behavior generally ascribed to those addicted to other drugs. They're responsible employees who come to work each day, perform their tasks, and go home at night to their pipe and slippers. In this case, their pipe holds a pellet of mab and the woman who brings their supper is more beautiful than the Queen of Astrikhan. The supper she brings, whether porridge or a chunk of salt pork, has a flavor comparable to the finest of viands. They sleep on soft mattresses and scented sheets, not pallets of straw.

They live each in their own tiny palace beside which runs not a sewer, but a sparkling stream. Their lives are infinitely better than they were…and all because of mab.

"Unlike other addictive drugs, one does not develop a tolerance for mab. A single dose taken each night lasts until the next night. True, the effect diminishes over the following day, but it makes one's labors less harsh. Rather than debilitating the addict, mab encourages him to take care of himself, to nurture his body. He now has reason to live, whereas with opium he hopes at best to survive and, truly, places a low value on survival. One might surmise that mab disposes the addict toward this cast of mind. What would you call a chemical compound that achieves those ends? That treats the worst symptoms of a community and causes it to function more smoothly? That makes its citizens content with their lot? Is it a drug, or is it a tonic? I say a tonic. In fact, that is how I've begun to market the drug in Port Chantay."

Councilman Rooney puffed himself up to full bloat and said, "Sir, you are the Devil."

"The Devil is never far from any of us, sir. Yet I'll wager I am closer to God than the priests who will soon inhabit the palace you're building at the end of the square."

"I've had a stomachful of this!" Rooney said; then, addressing the table: "Must we listen to more of his spew?"

A mild voice responded, "Oh, I think we should hear him out."

From the way the others reacted to the the man who had spoken, the youngest of the councilmen, Jean-Daniel Breque, turning toward him like dogs that have heard a piercing whistle, Rosacher understood that he had misread the council's dynamic. Councilman Breque was a small, sturdily built man with a largish head, a professorial beard shot through by a few gray threads, and wire spectacles. He seemed bemused by the proceedings, but it was evident that his bemusement had less to do with Rosacher's proposal than with the general reaction to it.

"You make a cogent point," he said to Rosacher. "But there are spiritual issues to be considered, are there not?"

"If by spiritual you're referring to the sensibilities of the Church...yes. The Church is a powerful concern. They must be paid their tribute. That said, permit me to ask you this. Where was the Church three years ago? Ten years ago? Fifty years ago? The sole reason for their interest in Teocinte is that it has become worth their while to put a franchise here. Now that there's an economy they can tap into, they're suddenly appalled by the sorry state of our souls. My word on it, should you write a law that criminalizes mab, they'll come to you and say, 'Let's be tolerant now. We don't want the poor to be flung down from their heaven, illusory though it may be. Give us time to work our magic, to wean them from the drug and redirect their loyalties, and we will rid you of Rosacher in due course.' They're no different from me. They're a business that offers consolation as a product…only theirs is an inferior product. They want to be paid and they'll take the money wherever they find it, even from a competitor. So I'll pay them and that moral outrage you're hearing now will be greatly muted."

"I take it your concern over the Church's past whereabouts was yet another rhetorical question," said Breque, and smiled.

Rosacher inclined his head to acknowledge this small joke made at his expense.

"If you believe all of this," said Breque, "then why respond to our summons? You must have a pressing reason for coming here this morning. Is there something you would have us do?"

"I want you to help protect your greatest resource," Rosacher said.

"Mangos? Silver? Somehow I don't think you have either of those in mind."

"Before I tell you more, I would like you to have at look at some figures."

Rosacher began passing out the papers Ludie had given him, laying a sheet in front of each councilman. Rooney sniffed and pushed his away.

"As you can see, the figures on the top half of the page reflect my month-by-month profits for the past year." Rosacher gave them a moment to study the figures. "You'll note the steady geometric increase."

"And this figure at the bottom, what does it represent?" asked Febres-Cordero.

"My estimated earnings for next year," said Rosacher. "Expenses have yet to be determined. They will undoubtedly rise in keeping with expansion."

"This much?" Savedra looked at him in astonishment. "Surely that can't be right?"

"My bookkeeper assures me that it's a most conservative estimate."

Rosacher noticed that Rooney was now studying his sheet of paper.

"Where do you keep your money?" asked Paltz.

"In a bank at Port Chantay. It's more secure than the local bank."

"From this I gather that you consider yourself to be our greatest resource," said Breque.

"Yes, I do. One of them," said Rosacher.

"And the other?"

"Griaule."

"Ah, yes. Griaule's blood is the active ingredient in mab, is it not?"

"It is," said Rosacher. "The process by which it is refined is the key to creating the drug, and that process is known only to myself and my partner."

"And who might that be?" Savedra asked.

"A man who wishes that his name not be divulged," said Rosacher. "But to the point, gentlemen. I would like you to levy a tax on my business. Say, five percent of my net profits annually. Such a tax would validate my business as a legal entity and grant me the protections of the law."

"Five percent of your gross would be more persuasive," said Rooney.

"The precise figure can be negotiated at another time," said Rosacher. "What I'm after today, if possible, is an agreement in principle."

He turned to his chair and found that Arthur was sitting in it. The giant made as though to stand, but Rosacher gestured for him to keep his seat and stood behind him.

"There is one more thing I want to propose," he said. "As you're aware, Mister Honeyman has organized a security force to safeguard my interests. I would like to expand that force into a militia…with your participation, of course. The day is coming when cities more powerful than ours will grow envious of Teocinte's prosperity and attempt to pirate my process and take control of the dragon. We need to be prepared against that day. I would be willing to fund the militia, but it would benefit your peace of mind, I think, if you were to share that burden, both as to costs and the constituency of the force. I propose that you appoint someone from your ranks to administer the militia. A general, if you will. He would oversee its functioning, the purchase of materiel and so forth, and would decide matters of policy. A militia further requires a general in the field, someone skilled in the art of war, someone who has the ability to train the men and lead them. I can think of no one more qualified for the post than Mister Honeyman."

Arthur glanced up at him, but quickly hid his startled expression and fixed the council members with his terrible smile. Palz, who had appeared on the verge of raising an objection, held his peace.

"It's an intriguing proposition." Breque clasped his hands, resting his forearms on the table. "And the picture you paint is a tempting one. A prosperous town, a contented populace, and, if your business continues to thrive, everyone in this room will become wealthy and powerful."

"You've no idea how wealthy," Rosacher said. "We've barely scratched the surface of what is possible. Consider how many other substances helpful to humankind may be found within Griaule's body."

"As I said, an intriguing proposal, though one that veers dangerously close to bribery. I have little doubt that you would be capable of achieving your goals under ordinary circumstances, but these circumstances are far from ordinary. When we were elected to the council, we swore an oath whose primary dictate was that we would do everything in our power to destroy Griaule. Now you ask us to protect him. The gap between the two positions is, I'm afraid, unbridgeable. Were we were to accept your proposal, we'd be thrown out of office."

The faces of the other council members displayed morose agreement.

Rosacher was caught short for a response; he had not predicted this. "Griaule..." he said, and pretended to clear his throat, searching for a logical avenue to pursue. "Griaule has permitted me to draw his blood. This is a certain sign that my purposes are in accord with his."

"That changes nothing," Breque said. "It is not the council's purpose to do Griaule's bidding."

"Yet you insist that he controls you, that his will is dominant. If that is true, you do his bidding whether or not you admit to it."

"For the sake of our dignity, if nothing else, we believe we are allowed a modicum of free will."

"You can't base your decisions on a bastardized ontology," said Rosacher. "Either Griaule controls you, or this notion of the dragon as god is ridiculous."

Struck by an idea, he once again pretended to clear his throat, stalling while he constructed his argument. Breque inquired whether he wanted a glass of water.

"How long have you been trying to kill Griaule?" Rosacher asked after taking a drink.

"There were countless attempts made before our body was organized, most of them ill-considered, a good many of them harebrained," said Savedra. "The first official attempt under aegis of the council was undertaken approximately six hundred years ago. Of course in the early days, the council was appointed by a feudal duke and had no real power. But as it's presently configured, more than two hundred years."

"I'm forced to assume, then, that Griaule is not ready to die," Rosacher said. "Or that you've failed miserably in satisfying your oath. If I wanted to kill the dragon, I'd cut down the forest in the hills close by him, pile the wood around his sides and set him on fire. Has that been tried?"

"Two centuries ago," said Febres-Cordero. "A strong wind blew the fire back on the town. They had to rebuild completely. It was an event that coincided with the removal of the feudal duke."

"We've explored every method we can think of," said Breque. "This explains why we've offered a reward and are entertaining more eccentric schemes."

"Yes, I met one of your eccentrics in the vestibule," Rosacher said. "A fellow by the name of Cattanay. He intends to paint a mural on the dragon's side using poisoned paint. Paint with a high lead or arsenic content. His expectation is that it will kill Griaule within several decades."

Rooney chuckled and Paltz shook his head, as if astounded by this foolishness, and said, "Well, it won't take several decades for us to deal with him!"

"Cattanay believes the process of painting will be too subtle for Griaule to recognize as an attempt to kill him. And by the time he does, if he does, he'll be too ill to remedy it. His control will have slipped. I think the plan may have some actual merit, but that's for you to decide." Rosacher fixed his gaze on Breque. "More pertinent to the question before you, a plan like Cattanay's, one that will take decades to achieve a result, would serve our mutual purposes. In thirty years we'll have made enough money to provide for our heirs to the tenth generation, and—theoretically, at any rate—you'll have a dead dragon, a booming economy, and a well-trained army. You've been at this for six centuries, gentlemen. I suspect your constituents won't quarrel overmuch with a plan that delays their gratification a few more years."

"Your argument presupposes that the plan will work," said Savedra. "What if it doesn't? Griaule may be capable of sniffing out Cattanay's intentions."

"You won't know that until you've tried," Rosacher said. "However, the signal virtue of Cattanay's plan is that he'll need three or four years to map out the project, build scaffolding, and so on. That should give you time to come up with an alternative. In the meantime we will profit and the town will thrive."

The faces of the men at the table were a comical study in perplexity and concentration. Rosacher made a gesture of finality. "Gentlemen, I've stated my case and now I have business to attend. With your kind permission, I'll leave you to your deliberations."

"If there are no further questions…" Breque looked inquiringly to the other councilmen. "Mister Rosacher, you have our thanks for making most exhilarating what otherwise might have been a tiresome adversarial experience. You can be sure that we will discuss every facet of what you have said. Give us a few days. You will hear from us by Friday at the latest." He beamed at Rosacher and gestured toward the door. "Would you mind telling Mister Cattanay to come in? I, for one, am eager to hear the details of his proposal."

As Rosacher and Arthur strode down the hill, Rosacher's mind went to the day ahead. There were appointments, contracts to examine, and he had to inspect repairs made to the refrigeration unit at the new factory. He would be fortunate to finish by seven o'clock. The time had come, he thought, to hire someone, perhaps several someones, to manage the business. Now that the council had been dealt with and, from his reading of Breque, he was confident of the result, he needed to get on with his study of the blood. He had been so consumed with the business that he had done pitifully little toward that end, and he looked forward to spending days locked away in a laboratory. But it was difficult to find people who were both competent and trustworthy. He would have to recruit his management staff on the coast and that meant a trip to Port Chantay, rounds of interviews…more time wasted. He despaired of creating a gap in his schedule.

"Pardon me, sir." Arthur's face was etched with worry. "What you said back there…that I was an expert on warfare. I don't know the first thing about it."

"There are dozens of books on the subject," Rosacher said impatiently. "You have wonderful instincts as to aggression. I'm sure you'll be a quick study."

"I can make out letters and sound some words, but..."

"Don't tell me you can't read?"

"Take me forever to read a book, it would. Even then, I reckon I might not make much sense of it."

"Learn, then," said Rosacher, a nasty edge on his voice, fuming inwardly over the incompetence with which he was surrounded. "If you don't learn, Arthur, how will you ever advance yourself?"

5

SHORTLY AFTER EIGHT O'CLOCK that evening, Rosacher arrived at Ludie's apartments. He hesitated, debating whether or not to knock, ultimately deciding that since he was attempting to restore intimacy, he should behave as would an intimate—he opened the door. The room was dimly lit by a single ornamental floor lamp in a corner, its flame turned low, and the windows held rectangles of purplish dusk. Walls and ceiling were draped in swaths of billowy, diaphanous cloth—pastel shades of green, yellow and blue that shrank the enclosed space and was intended to make the room appear to be the interior of a tent. Beneath this canopy, pillows and rugs were arranged about a teak table on which a cold supper was laid. The decor represented an ideal of luxury in Ludie's homeland, or rather what she presumed to be an ideal—she had been born into poverty and sold at the age of six to a brothel-keeper from Peppertree; he in turn had sold her to the Hotel San Salida.

Rosacher collapsed amidst the pillows, closed his eyes and was assailed by nagging concerns relating to business. Attempting to quiet his mind, he sank deeper into a morass of petty entanglements, expenditures, collections and whatnot. When he succeeded in pushing these matters into the background, the question of his three-year lapse arose, and that so disturbed him, he abandoned the idea of resting, opened his eyes and saw Ludie standing above him. She was dressed to match the décor, wearing a gauzy peignoir that revealed the voluptuous contours of her body; yet in opposition to the seductive image she presented, her expression was one of poorly concealed distaste.

"I apologize for being late," he said. "I..."

"How did you fare with the council?" She reclined beside him on the opposite side of the table and popped a slice of orange into her mouth. "It must have gone well or else you would have been too preoccupied to come at all."

He told her in brief what had been said within the council chamber and she said flatly, "Congratulations."

"You don't sound like you mean it."

"Oh, but I do!" Iciness slipped into her voice. "I've never doubted you, Richard. You're far more accomplished a criminal than ever you were a scientist."

"This is good news for both of us," he said, electing not to respond in kind, not wanting to alienate her further. "You're certainly due your share of congratulations. The plan was *our* plan, not mine alone, and I would never have had the gumption to carry it through without your support."

"You sound as if you're speaking at a testimonial dinner. Do I get a gold watch, too?" Her laugh was brittle, a single disparaging note.

"This Cattanay," she went on. "Do you think it wise to allow him to proceed with his plans? What if the poison works more swiftly than he anticipates?"

"I'll stop him before he can do any real harm. With Arthur in position at the head of the militia, no one will be able to thwart us. Until then, Cattanay's project is of such scope, it'll deflect attention."

He heard people talking in the street below and the crazed yapping of a dog, abruptly cut off and replaced by a whimper. Her flowery scent seemed to intensify; her eyes, large and dark and liquid, appeared lit from within.

"Aren't you hungry?" she asked.

"I thought I was, but...no."

Following another patch of silence, she said, "Well..." She sat up and undid the fastening of the peignoir, letting it slip from her shoulders to reveal a breast. When he displayed no reaction, she lifted a breast and made a lascivious show of licking her nipple, keeping her eyes on him all the while.

"Stop it!" he said angrily.

Dropping into the patois she had once used with her clientele at the brothel, she said teasingly, "You mus be a jumbie mon, you don wan to slip-slide wit this fine gyal."

"Stop!"

She stared at him heatedly. "Isn't this what you wanted?"

"What I wanted..." He gave his head a violent shake, frustrated by her misreading of him. "Yes, that's part of it, but I wanted more, I wanted..."

"Would you like me to fetch another woman? Perhaps the two of us could please you."

"That's not what I meant by 'more.'"

She watched dispassionately as he positioned himself cross-legged on the pillows.

"We were friends once, weren't we, Ludie? More than friends. We used to talk for hours, we..." Rosacher made a fist, as if he intended to pound on something; then he relaxed his fingers and lowered his hand. "I hoped we could go back to how things were."

"Then you're a fool, Richard. It's sweet in a way. It's all that's left of the boy I met in Morningshade. And you *were* a boy. You had a boy's passion, a boy's reckless-ness. But your passion has changed into a lust for wealth, and your recklessness has matured into ruthlessness. You don't see that in yourself. You'll pay it lip service, you'll admit to it. But you don't really see it and so you remain a fool."

Full darkness had fallen—the windowpanes like black semaphore flags salted with a message of stars. She had spoken with such mildness that her characterization of him had the tenor of sage counsel.

"I love you," Rosacher said.

"No, you had a feeling. Your brain sparked and you had a feeling. You said to yourself, I've got to get back with Ludie, back to how things used to be. Even though how you thought things were, that truly wasn't how they were. You know that, but you want to deny it. You want to hold onto that feeling, because it's the only one you've had lately that has nothing to do with business."

Everything she said diminished him. He thought that if she kept talking, he would wind up the size of a homunculus, a tiny man sitting on a vast pillow, a plush island upon which he'd been marooned.

"I'm a fool, too," she said. "There was a time I thought I loved you. I knew all the love in me had been dragged out and kicked into the street, but I hung onto that thought. Love was something I could dream about whenever sone foul-smelling bastard was riding me. It was a story I'd been told. A fairytale. But I couldn't hold on for long. It passed...and your feeling will pass as well. In a week you'll be consumed with something else."

"We're friends, though, aren't we?" Rosacher said. "We're at least friends."

"We have a bond, but..."

"Yes?"

"I owe you everything, Richard. My life. Money. Freedom." She tapped the side of her head. "You taught me how to use this, and how to behave like a lady. I'm grateful for that. It's why I stay. But for that very reason, because *you* did everything, because *you* lifted me up from Morningshade, I can't help resenting you. I still feel owned, owing you so much, and that feeling trumps friendship."

"That's absurd. You don't owe me a thing, and you don't have to stay. I can get someone else to manage the books."

A wounded look crossed her face. It pleased him to recognize that he could yet hurt her, that she was not without emotion where he was involved.

"I'll stay until it's right to leave. And when I go, it won't be farther away than the other side of the hill, where I won't have to look at that damned lizard every time I step out the door."

She reached between two pillows, withdrew a lacquered box and put it on the table; she removed from it a pipe with a long, straight stem and a brass bowl, the image of a miniature dragon raised on its surface. "This is what you want. To touch that night again, the night Arthur came into our lives. I think it's what we both want. Things have gotten crinkly between us and this is what we need to straighten it all out."

"Thank you, no."

Ludie packed the bowl with a bed of moist tobacco. "Have you forgotten how to play?" She embedded a grayish white pellet of mab in the tobacco. "I think you have. I think you forgot the instant the idea for the business came into your head. One minute you were the Richard I knew. A sweet, intemperate boy. The next, you were acting smooth as a bishop on Sunday morning. Can't nothing catch on you now, you're so smooth."

She took a match from the box, ignited it with the nail of her thumb, and lit the pipe. Her cheeks hollowed as she drew in smoke. She leaned back amid the pillows, letting smoke trickle out between her parted lips. "Ohh..." she said breathily, and gave a delicate shudder. She closed her eyes for a second and drew in more smoke. After a third lungful, she looked as if she filled out her skin more thoroughly, as if she had ripened all in a moment. Her eyes were brighter, a'dance with gleams.

"Touch me," she said, lightly slurring.

With reluctance, for part of him, the lesser part, wanted to resist this fake, this chemical fraud, he gloved the side of her breast, rubbing the nipple in a circular motion with the ball of his thumb. Her eyelids fluttered down and she bit her lower lip and made a musical noise, barely audible, a noise with which he was most familiar, though he had not heard it for many months. To hear it now affected him strangely. It raised the flag of his desire, yet he also felt a chill, as if her arousal endangered him. She caught his hand, brought it to her mouth and licked the tip of his forefinger. In her face he saw the refinements of love—her features had softened, her gaze was doting, her manner one of fervid devotion.

"Richard..." she said, leaving the remainder of the sentence unspoken, yet not unheeded.

A horse and rider went by on the street, the percussive sound of its hooves fading to muted pops. Shamed by his weakness, Rosacher picked up the pipe.

6

HAT NIGHT ROSACHER DREAMED of a cavernous room with a slight curvature to its ceiling, so long that neither end was visible. Upon the walls of the room flowed the black-on-gold patterns of Griaule's blood, like the cryptic symbols written by God upon a serpent's scales, seeming characters in a long-forgotten script. And perhaps it was the dragon's bloodstream in which he stood, unaffected by its currents, breathing without difficulty, altogether comfortable and calm, for whenever he shifted about the patterns rippled and distorted as if his movement had disturbed a liquid medium. He tried to focus on the pattern, to track a single shape as it changed and changed again. To his bewilderment, one of the shapes straightened and grew larger, resolving into an anthropomorphic figure that approached him at a brisk pace. A man, judging by the size, yet Rosacher assumed him to be a preternatural creature. As the man drew near, Rosacher saw that his hands were wrapped in bandages and he was attired in a black suit with an unfashionably long jacket. Another bandage obscured the left side of his face and a slouch hat with its brim turned down shadowed his features, subduing a tangle of graying hair. There was no chair, yet he sat and crossed his legs as if there were a chair beneath him, one fashioned of the flowing black-and-gold blood.

"Hello, Richard," he said at length in a grating voice.

Rosacher, startled to hear him speak, stepped backward, slipped and would have fallen had not the blood supported him, forming a cushion-like surface into which he sank.

"What is this place?" Rosacher asked, struggling to sit up—the pillowy stuff beneath him was so slick, he had difficulty achieving a stable position.

The man chuckled.

"We're inside Griaule, are we not?" asked Rosacher, glancing about, searching for some further clue to substantiate the notion.

"In one way or another, we are always inside Griaule," said the man. "On the brightest day, we are part of his shadow."

This declaration bore the stamp of an oft-repeated phrase and Rosacher bridled at it, as he would at anything that smacked of zealotry.

"Who are you?" he demanded

"A messenger."

"Have we met? You appear to know me."

"We have a minimal acquaintance, yet I doubt you would acknowledge it. But I know you well enough, though I had forgotten how callow you were."

The man loosed a terrible, racking cough that doubled him over. On recovering, he fussed with his lapels and smoothed down the fabric of his trousers, as if worried lest they wrinkle.

"Be careful when next you wake," he said, wheezing, his voice raspier than before. "Do not react to anything you may hear or see. Don't cry out for help. Slip from the bed as quietly as you can. Your enemies are near."

"Am I asleep now?"

"You are, yet this is no dream. Heed my warning or you will not see daybreak."

"If not a dream, what is it? A sending of some kind?"

"Don't be preoccupied with the nature of the experience. Listen to me!"

The man was possessed by a second coughing fit, of longer duration than the first, and Rosacher volunteered to examine him if he so wished, saying that the cough suggested some deep-seated malady.

"It's nothing," said the man, struggling for breath. "Did you hear what I told you to do?"

"Yes. Don't say anything. Slip from my bed."

"Quietly!"

"Yes, yes. I understand. Quietly. I'd see to that cough if I were you."

It occurred to Rosacher that it was the height of idiocy to offer medical advice to someone who might be a figment of his imagination, yet he inquired of the man as to what portion of reality he might represent. Was he an embodiment of the dragon, the image sent to deliver a message, or a living person co-opted for that purpose? And how had he acquired this foreknowledge of his, Rosacher's, fate?

"Were I to answer 'yes' to your first two questions, I would not be far off the mark," the man said. "Your third question requires a more complicated answer. Though he was once a mortal creature, long-lived yet born to die, Griaule has grown not only in size, but also in scope. Demiurge may be too great a word to describe him, but he is akin to such a presence. An incarnation, if you will. His flesh has become one with the earth. He knows its every tremor and convulsion. His thoughts roam across the plenum, and his mind is a cloud that encompasses our world. His blood..." He made a florid gesture that seemed to include the entire surround. "His blood is the marrow of time. Centuries and days flow through him, leaving behind a residue that he incorporates into his being. Is it any wonder that he knows our fates?"

"Nonsense," Rosacher said, annoyed by the man's unctuous certitude. "Griaule is a lizard. A monumental lizard who may possess some potency, an ability to influence the weak-minded; but he is nonetheless a lizard and thus mortal. He bleeds, he breathes, and he will die."

"He will die when he wishes to die," said the man. "As do all perfected souls who give their light to the world. But I came to warn you, not to debate philosophical matters."

"This is scarcely a debate. There is nothing at issue."

The man stood and studied Rosacher. "You are a fool, but in Griaule's design there is a place for fools. Do you not wonder why I was sent?"

"No more than I'm inclined to wonder about why my ass itches. I assume it's because of an irritation, something disagreeable that caused an adverse reaction."

The man shook his head ruefully and said, "I almost wish my warning would be in vain." He then gave a curt salute and strode off at the same rapid pace with which he had approached, merging with the other dark figures carried by the dragon's blood.

As unnerved by the man's abrupt exit as he had been by his advent, Rosacher called after him, not wishing to be alone in that solitude. When he did not reappear, Rosacher braced himself with the thought that the man might have proven even more annoying had he stayed. The patterns of the blood troubled his sight. He closed his eyes, yet continued to see them in his mind's eye and was seduced by their consistent flow, their ceaseless evolution and by the intimations he began to receive from them—shimmers of emotion, fragmentary landscapes, pieces of memory all, but memories that he did not recognize for his own, like the glints of ornamental carp glimpsed beneath the surface of a golden pond.

He woke into a pitch-dark room, rain driving against the walls of the house, a firm mattress and satin sheets beneath him, and had a sense of familiar enclosure. His room, his house. He fumbled for a candlestick, but recalled the man's warning. It was the height of the ridiculous to heed a warning voiced in a dream, and yet the dream had been so unusual in form and substance, he was compelled to give it credence. Holding his breath, he eased from beneath the covers. The floor was cold. He crept away from the bed, wary of creaking boards, and groped his way along the wall until he located a corner. He stood with his back pressed against the angle of the walls, and began to feel even more foolish for having obeyed the compulsion of a dream. A noise alerted him and he froze in place. A clock ticked, the rain drummed. The cold of the floor spread through his limbs, and then a flurry of noise came from the bed, sounding as if someone were taking a mallet to the pillows. Rosacher edged toward the door, groped for the knob, and was blinded by a dazzling light. His eyes adjusted and he made out a cowled figure kneeling on the bed, a shadowed face peering in his direction, a dagger in one hand and holding aloft in the other what looked to be a starry, blue-white gemstone, the source of the radiance.

The assassin sprang for him, a nightmare of flapping robes and an empty cowl. Rosacher was bowled over by the attack, but succeeded in grabbing the man's knife-arm, securing his wrist, and they went rolling across the carpet at the foot of the bed. For an instant Rosacher gained the upper hand, straddling the assassin, but the man whipped him onto his back—effortlessly, it seemed—and came astride him, forcing the dagger toward Rosacher's throat. The point of the blade scored his jaw. He cried out, a desperate shout, and sought to dislodge the assassin by bucking with his hips, directing his remaining energies toward diverting the blade. Light still issued from the gemstone fallen to the floor, but he could see nothing of his attacker's face. The assassin shifted his grip on the hilt of the dagger, relaxing downward pressure for a split-second, and Rosacher seized the opportunity to cry out again. The dagger nicked him twice more, once in the shoulder and once on the collarbone. He suffocated in the mustiness of the man's woolen robe, in the pepper-and-onions scent of his last meal. With a surge of energy, realizing he had no chance fighting from his back, Rosacher brought his knee up hard into the assassin's back, driving him forward, and scrambled from beneath him, regaining his feet, panting, gulping in air. The assassin came up into a crouch and feinted with the dagger...and then the door burst open, lantern-light cut the dimness, and three of Rosacher's servants rushed into the room. Hesitating but a moment, they leaped at the assassin and bore him to the floor. Arthur appeared in the doorway, pistol in hand, clad in a nightshirt that fell to his bony knees. Drained of his reserves, Rosacher staggered to the bed and sat. The assassin lay without struggling in the grip of the three men, one of whom had received a slash across the arm. His cowl had fallen back, revealing him to be a mere boy of sixteen or thereabouts, towheaded and with a baby-ish face. He seemed to be praying, his eyes shut, lips moving silently. Rosacher watched him without pity.

"It'll take more than prayer to bring you through this night," he said.

The boy's eyelids fluttered, but he continued to pray.

"Are you injured?" Arthur asked.

"Not badly." Rosacher pointed to the gemstone on the floor. "Here. Hand it to me."

Arthur scooped it up. "It's one of the Church's baubles."

The gem was warm to the touch, about the size of a peach, faceted on its uppermost surface. It no longer shone. After a cursory examination, Rosacher tossed it onto the bed.

"What are you doing here?" he asked Arthur.

The giant adopted a sheepish expression. "I was induced to stay by your new kitchen girl. Good thing, as it turned out."

"Where's Ludie?"

"I don't think she's back from her ride. She said she'd be gone 'til tomorrow."

A maid peeked in the door and Arthur told her to fetch bandages and ointment. Still unsteady, Rosacher stood and clung to the bedpost for support. Arthur asked once more if he was all right. Rosacher ignored the question and waved at the assassin. "Take him to the cellar and question him. And send someone to the barracks. I'll need a force of twenty men."

"What've you got in mind?"

"Just get them! And make certain they're men we can trust. Have them dress in civilian clothes." Rosacher indicated the three servants who were hustling the assassin from the room. "See that they get some money."

Once Arthur had gone, he went into the bathroom and lit the wall lamp. Memories crowded into his brain, new ones mixing with old, slotting into their rightful place, aligning with events, times, locations, and even before he looked into the mirror he knew that he had suffered a second and more substantial lapse of time. Six years! No, seven. Seven years. He was surprised by how greatly he had changed. His head was no longer shaven, his hair flecked with gray, curling down over his neck. His face was leaner, harsher, with deep lines beside the mouth and eyes. An imperious face, unadmitting of emotion. He found much to admire in that face. A new firmness was seated there, reflecting a pragmatic cast of mind—that must explain why he was not so disoriented as he had been on the previous occasion. He had grown more adaptable to change, though he could not adapt to the idea that years were being ripped away from him.

Blood trickled from the cut on his jaw and from another on his brow, running down his cheek and neck. A bloodstain mapped the right shoulder of his night-shirt. He took off the shirt and inspected the wounds to his shoulder and collarbone. They were shallow and both had nearly stopped bleeding. His anger had dissipated to a degree, but now it hardened and thrust up from his other emotions like a mountain peak from a sea of clouds. Although he was furious with the Church, who had undoubtedly sent the assassin, the greater portion of his outrage was reserved for himself and for the worlds, the knowledge that he had not conquered in the way he had desired...and for Griaule, the agency ultimately responsible for his travail and disappointment. No blow on the head could have caused this and he could no longer deny that a monstrous lizard ruled his fate. That Griaule had spared his life by sending a messenger gave him no comfort. He was, he thought, being preserved for some more intricate fate and he hungered for something, a spell, a spoonful of medicine, a prayer that would restore his lost years. His thoughts lashed about in frustration.

A tapping at the door diverted him and he yanked it open, preparing to vilify whomever it might be. The maid, her brown hair cropped short, broad-beamed and heavy-breasted, her dumpling face stamped with a common prettiness that would before long slump into matronly, double-chinned drabness...she bore ointment and bandages. As she applied the ointment, going about it with mute animal concentration, he felt an urge to re-establish control, to impose his will, and that urge combined with a less subtle desire. He fondled her breasts, an intimacy that did not cause her to complain. He might have been patting her on the head for all the reaction she displayed. Once she had done with the bandages, he bent her over the sink. She hiked up her skirts and diddled herself, making ready for him. Her bovine compliance irritated him and he spent the next ten or fifteen minutes trying to transform her stuporous expression into one that resembled passion. She hung her head and he ordered her to lift it so he could watch her face in the mirror. At length she closed her eyes and pressed her lips together and yielded up a thin squeal. He sent her from him, telling her to take a coin from atop the dresser, and—his confidence if not fully revived, then braced and polished—he threw on his clothes and went down to the cellar to determine what had been learned from the assassin.

7

O F ALL THE BUILDINGS atop Haver's Roost, the cathedral was the grandest and most graceful, a serene architecture of swoops and curves that made it appear as if the body of the building had been modeled after some natural shape—a nesting white dove, perhaps. Instead of the dove's neck and head, a blunt spire arose, forming at its peak the setting for a crystal the size of a small house, the mother of the gem carried by the assassin (these crystals were mined only in the caves underlying the Cathedral of the Lioness in far-off Mospiel, the seat of the church's authority, and a lavish ceremony accompanied their placement atop each new spire). Rather than looking out of place amid the less ambitious geometries of the government buildings, the cathedral seemed to knit them together, to be the altar before which they, the simple pews, were arranged.

The morning star had risen and the sky had lightened to a deep royal blue by the time Rosacher and his militia reached the church. He deployed half his men, armed with rifles and under an officer's direction, to watch the exits of the rectory attached to the rear of the church, and kept the remainder to guard the double doors at the front. Once the men were in position, he appropriated two lanterns and hurled them against the doors, an act that magnified his rage. Burning oil spattered the wood and soon the doors were ablaze. Arthur sent four men to guard the entrance to the square. Showing uncommon foresight, the city fathers had chosen to leave the entrance a narrow path between buildings that could barely funnel two men walking abreast into the square, thus permitting it to be easily defended against a mob. Rosacher doubted there would be more than token resistance to his actions, if that. In recent years the influence of the church, both in Teocinte and elsewhere, had been undercut by the popularity of mab.

The doors collapsed into a heap of burning boards and, calmer now that he had taken this step, Rosacher kicked them aside as he moved into the nave, catching sight of a priest jumping down from the altar and ducking into the corridor that led away into the rectory. Except for the chuckling of the flames at his back, all was silent and, though his attitude toward the Church was thoroughly cynical, he found the body of the cathedral daunting, with its formidable phalanxes of empty black pews and a ceiling illuminated by a mural that depicted the advent of the Gentle Beast (its image not shown, but its presence intimated by a wash of white light before which the lesser beasts, man included, bowed). Aisles carpeted in dark green channeled toward the altar, a stage set decorated in a medley of greens and sectioned off by velvet ropes behind which were displayed seven wooden thrones, each inlaid with a design of gold and lapis lazuli denoting its station; and above it all was suspended a crystal smaller than the one atop the spire, though not so small that it failed to light every corner of the cathedral. Even Arthur looked to be cowed by the setting, but he ordered the militiamen forward and, with Rosacher at their head, they advanced to the foot of the altar.

"Your assassin is dead!" shouted Rosacher. "Must I ferret you from your holes?"

He waited for a reply and, when none was forthcoming, he said, "I want to speak with Bishop Ruiz! I'll give you two minutes to send him out! Two minutes! Then I'll send in my men!"

Arthur eased up beside him. "What's the plan?"

"That's up to the bishop," said Rosacher.

"Burning down the doors of a church…it won't sit well with the prelates in Mospiel."

"What would you have me do? Kill them?"

"You can't trust 'em. Might as well be damned for stealing a crown as for stealing a penny."

"Perhaps I will kill them. But one should never act before one explores the possibilities for negotiation."

"I thought you were angry," Arthur said. "When I'm angry I don't think about nothing."

Rosacher grunted in amusement. "You may find that instructive."

A thin, dark priest in a brown robe, his skin a shade lighter than Ludie's, emerged from the door leading to the rectory. His crispy hair was turning gray, yet his features were those of a handsome man of middle years: wide, full lips, a broad nose and a high forehead.

"Good morning, Bishop," said Rosacher. "I apologize for disturbing your sleep, but then mine was disturbed this night...and most rudely."

"If you leave now I may be able to intercede with you before the Beast," Ruiz said sternly.

He drew himself up, possibly preparing to deliver a vow or an imprecation, but Rosacher stepped into the gap and said, "Put to rest any notion that your animist claptrap has any hold on me. Surely a man who has been in the religion business for as long as you can recognize a confirmed skeptic? I recognize you as such, so let's do away with pretense and see if we can devise a circumstance that will guarantee your safety beyond morning."

Ruiz was stoic, yet his anxiety seemed to stir the air. "I will not speak with you so long as your men occupy the church."

Rosacher ordered the militiamen to withdraw and, once they were out of earshot, he said, "There. No witnesses save for Arthur, and you may think of him as an interested party to our conversation."

"You dare much," said Ruiz. "Do you know the force that will be brought against you for this night's work? Once news of your sacrilege reaches Mospiel, they will move swiftly."

"The news may never reach Mospiel," said Rosacher. "At least in no form that you would sanction."

With a florid gesture he invited the bishop to sit with him in the front pew. Arthur leaned against the altar rail.

"I've been speculating on the effect that a weakened church may have upon my enterprise for some time now," said Rosacher. "I presumed the waning of the church's influence would be good for business, but I didn't anticipate the swiftness with which it would wane. Nor did I expect the church would be moved to acts of desperation. I take it the order for the assassination originated with that old fart in Mospiel?"

Ruiz maintained a stiff silence.

Rosacher made a frustrated noise. "There's no point to your obstinacy. The boy has confesssed."

"If you already know the answer," said Ruiz, "why ask the question?"

"I wish to confirm that His High Holiness issued the order and not you. It will make a significant difference in my handling of the situation."

Ruiz deliberated for a matter of seconds and returned a minimal nod. "I have no voice in such decisions."

"Why send a boy to do the job?" asked Rosacher. "Is the Church's opinion of me so low?"

"Understand that I was against this from the outset. My opinion aside, they had used the boy previously. He was adjudged competent."

"Well," Rosacher said. "He's no longer capable of competence, let me assure you."

"They?" said Arthur. "Not we?"

"I deemed it unnecessary," Ruiz said. "When measured against the life of the church, the life of one man is transitory and unimportant. Even should you live out your natural span, you'll die soon enough."

"Most reasonable," said Rosacher. "But mab will continue to be produced long after I die."

Ruiz sniffed. "People tire of perfection."

"A verity that likely explains the longevity of the church."

Ruiz refrained from comment.

"I suppose we could debate whose drug is superior," said Rosacher. "But our time might be better spent in coming up with a strategy that will allow the two to co-exist."

"Are you toying with me?"

"Not at all."

"I don't believe you. I'm told you're the kind of predator who likes to lick his prey all over before biting them in half. I refuse to engage in the process."

"Whom have I bitten in half recently?"

Ruiz turned from Rosacher and sat facing the green-and-gold depth of the altar.

"You won't talk to me?" Rosacher asked. "Even though it may be to your advantage?"

The bishop closed his eyes and sighed.

"I'll talk, then." Rosacher crossed his legs and leaned back. "Almost fifty years ago the church convened a council to determine whether or not Griaule should be included in its pantheon. Not surprisingly, the decision was a narrow one in favor of the status quo. I'm of the opinion that the council should be re-convened to study the question anew."

It appeared that Ruiz was about to speak, but he pressed his lips together and maintained his silence.

"But I'm getting ahead of myself," Rosacher went on. "If war should arise from what I've done this morning—and the Church has prosecuted wars with much less provocation—it will be long and costly. I control the militia and the city council. I can promise you that Teocinte will defend itself vigorously no matter how great a force is brought against it. Yet this can all be averted by a simple negotiation."

"People have also warned me against your negotiations," Ruiz said.

"Then you are forearmed, are you not?"

The bishop inclined his head. "Do you have a proposal?"

"I do. In exchange for a cessation of hostilities between the Church and myself, I am willing, after the passage of twenty-five years, to hand over all factories and business connections, all my stock, everything relating to the production and sale of mab. Further, I'll reveal the process by which the drug is refined. In the interim, I'll cease my ranting about the church."

Ruiz looked at him askance. "That seems rather one-sided. Why would you capitulate to this extent?"

"I'm already wealthy," said Rosacher. "In twenty-five years I'll be obscenely wealthy. Within a decade mab will be but a minor portion of my business interests and so, in return for what will be inconsequential to me, I'll have peace of mind. I'll never entirely trust you, of course, but I will trust that you won't raise an army against me."

"Perhaps we should have sent an assassin years ago," Ruiz said with a half-smile.

"I wasn't prepared to make this offer years ago," said Rosacher. "I am now. Will you convey my proposal to Mospiel?"

"What surety can you provide that you'll reveal the refining process?"

"The same you can provide me that there'll be no future attempts on my life. None. A certain amount of trust is implicit in every bargain. But you will have a legal document certifying the transferal of my stocks of mab to the Church. That alone will profit you enormously."

"Very well," Ruiz said after a pause. "I'll pass along the proposal. I imagine Mospiel will be sufficiently interested to send an emissary who will judge whether or not you're a reasonable man. He'll be someone with the authority to negotiate the particulars of an agreement."

"Excellent! I look forward to speaking with him."

Ruiz adopted a more relaxed posture. "This business of a re-convened council? What does that have to do with the agreement we've discussed?"

"We'll need an explanation for the burnt doors. Since people tend to blame the weather on Griaule, why not blame him for this? Or credit him?"

"Credit him with violating the sanctity of the Church?"

"If the Church intends to associate itself with a product that incorporates the dragon's blood, it would be foolish to demonize him further. It would be helpful, as I said, if the church convened a council to revisit the question of Griaule's divinity. They needn't reach any conclusion. Merely convening such a body will send a signal that will be impossible to ignore."

"I see your point, but what excuse can there be for burning down the doors of a church? How can it be painted as a righteous act?"

"Two prostitutes were murdered in Morningshade last week. Isn't that right, Arthur?"

"Aye. Chopped into bits, they were," the giant said.

"And the murderer escaped without being identified, did he not?"

"That he did. He wore a hooded cape and none saw his face. It's said he were a traveler in ladies' apparel, but there's no proof of that. At any rate, I wager he's long gone from Teocinte."

"There's your excuse," Rosacher said to Ruiz. "The murderer sought refuge in the church. Griaule, aware of this as he is of all things, became so outraged that he sent a wisp of his fiery breath to point the way. I'll leave it to you to provide the miraculous details. You're more versed at it than I."

"Your men," said Ruiz. "They witnessed the event."

"They're good lads," said Arthur. "They know how to hold their tongues. They'll bear witness to whatever they're told to."

"As, I'm sure, will your priests," Rosacher said. "And if we both stand behind the story, who's to gainsay us?"

Ruiz rested the point of his chin atop his clasped hands and nodded. "It's very neat. I can see no flaw. None that would be an impediment, at any rate." His smile seemed the article of an oily complicity. "Everyone expects a loose end or two where religious matters are concerned."

"It's settled, then?"

"I can't speak for Mospiel, but once they've studied your proposal I have little doubt that they'll seize the opportunity to enter into an agreement."

"Very well, then!" Rosacher stood and clapped him on the shoulder. "Now all we need is a priest to stand in for the murderer."

Ruiz gaped at him.

"The common folk loves their executions," said Arthur. "They don't never feel so right as when someone's dancing the Devil's Jig."

"Do you have a true believer among your priests?" Rosacher asked. "Someone young and naïve who'll perceive his sacrifice as necessary for the good of the Church?"

"It's best when they go to the gallows all pale and stricken," Arthur said. "It don't really matter if they proclaim their innocence. People's blood is up and they'd drop the trapdoor on his High Holiness himself just to watch his heels kick."

Ruiz's expression swerved between outrage and bewilderment.

"Surely you didn't think this gain would come without some trivial cost?" Rosacher asked.

"Trivial? You call a man's life trivial?"

"I believe you yourself expressed a similar idea," said Rosacher. He pretended to search his memory. "How did you put it? Something about the life of one man…"

Ruiz came to his feet. "I'll have nothing to do with this!"

"Your participation would facilitate matters, but it's scarcely essential. I will, through some agency, succeed in gaining the prelate's ear. You might consider how it will go for you when Mospiel learns of your reluctance to pass on a lucrative offer. I understand you have friends in high places, but the church has been uniformly repressive of those who stand in the way of its profit. I feel certain they would thwart any ambitions you harbor with regard toward advancement in the hierarchy. And that may be the least consequence of their displeasure."

"But why a priest? Surely you can find a more credible scapegoat? "

Arthur stepped to Rosacher's side. "Would you prefer we plucked some poor lad out of Morningshade?"

"Because I want you to bleed," said Rosacher. "Apart from that, it will go down well with the citizenry. Your priests are commonly seen in the brothels, and there is resentment over the fact that they proclaim themselves pure while wallowing in the same mire as do ordinary men. Such a sacrifice will help the church's reputation more than it will impeach it. Imagine the sermons you'll be able to preach. You can exult in your shame, make a pageant of public humiliation. It will humanize Mospiel, set a penitent face atop its bloated body. But you must decide now. I won't waste more time on this. Should you choose to die a martyr to the cause, my men have work to do."

"Would you condone such a slaughter?" asked Ruiz, appearing shaken. "How can you possibly profit from it?"

"Fewer priests, for one," said Arthur.

Flatly, without a trace of sarcasm, Rosacher said, "What are the lives of a handful of priests when measured against the good of the Church?"

"What choice do I have?" Ruiz waved weakly in the direction of the rectory. "Take whomever you wish."

"No, no," said Rosacher. "The process of selection should be an informed one. We'll leave that little chore to you."

Ruiz said, "I'll do as you ask."

"We'll just wait here whilst you make your selection, shall we?" Arthur showed his teeth in a horrid grin.

"This may take some time," said Ruiz. "I'll have to…"

"I'm aware of your methods," Rosacher said. "You need to console, to comfort, to offer assurances of a place beside the Beast in his eternal kingdom. We'll be patient while you work your magic."

Ruiz walked stiffly toward the rectory door, but then he turned, his face knotted in fury. "You bastard! You…"

"I know, I know," said Rosacher mildly. "But you *were* warned."

8

T HE TOWER THAT MERIC Cattanay had erected so
he might observe the progress of his great work
was a rickety affair some eighty feet high, so
hastily carpentered of boards and poles that a strong wind
would sway it, threatening to send it crashing down onto
the rooftops and smoking chimneys of Morningshade
below. From a platform at the summit, it afforded one
an unimpeded view of the painting on the dragon's side
(albeit one complicated by scaffolding and the dozen or
so artisans currently occupying it) and of the painting—
it appeared to Rosacher's eyes as a blotch of gold a few
shades lighter than the dragon's natural color, spreading
from the middle joint of the foreleg around the curve of
the side. Other colors were beginning to emerge from the

blotch, but gave no hint of the image that would one day be presented. Also visible against the gray morning sky were the enormous vats that had been constructed atop Griaule's flat forehead. In these, the raw materials that produced the poisoned paint were distilled. Smoke rose from beneath them at every hour of the day and night, making it seem that the dragon was venting frustration through his skull.

Rosacher had climbed the tower in order to be alone (an ambition thwarted when he discovered Cattanay, bearded and bedraggled, sketching on the platform) and to gain perspective, though not on the painting. He had taken to sleeping as little as possible, doing everything in his power to stay awake, yet some sleep was essential and he had woken that morning to discover he had lost another four years—at this rate he calculated that he had at best another week or so to live, and he hoped this elevated position would lend itself to a fresh comprehension of the problem. After a brief exchange of pleasantries, Cattanay, who seemed as perturbed by Rosacher's presence as was Rosacher with his, returned to his sketching, and Rosacher sat on the lip of the platform, dangling his legs off the side, staring at the golden blotch. His thoughts were in disarray and resisted all attempts to marshal them. He kept coming back to the panicked recognition that he was now, as best he could determine, forty-three years old, and that the better part of sixteen years had been stripped from him. The obvious thing to do would be to stop moping and get to work on his study of the blood and hope that it led to an insight into his current difficulties. He had built a laboratory in his factory and nothing stood in his way...unless it was Griaule. Not for the first time, it occurred to him that he must have been close to achieving a breakthrough, one detrimental to the dragon's health or contrary to his schemes, for Griaule to have intervened and set his life upon such a different course. This inspired him to go forward with his researches, but the idea that Griaule might thwart him at any second neutered the impulse. And, too, he wondered if he still retained the discipline to stare for hours into a microscope. Ludie was probably right—he made a more successful criminal than he did a scientist.

Boards creaked behind him and, turning, he saw Cattanay sitting cross-legged, unwrapping a sandwich from a packet of brown paper. Glancing up, he offered half to Rosacher, who declined. Cattanay took a bite, chewed with gusto and swallowed. He made a contented sound and brushed crumbs from his beard.

"This cheese is excellent," he said. "You should try it. Allie, my companion, soaks it in an infusion of berries. Quite tasty."

Again Rosacher declined. He watched the artist eat for several seconds and then, feeling awkward with the silence, he asked how the work was going.

Cattanay shrugged. "It goes and it goes. I've been unable to manufacture a proper magenta. The color changes so much on the scales..." He gestured with the sandwich. "We'll get it right sooner or later."

"I meant to ask if you had any idea of how long Griaule can survive?"

"Haven't a clue. Sorry. I suppose he could pop off any old time. You need to ask an expert in dragon physiology...if there are such. You were a doctor once, no? You're more qualified than I to give an opinion."

Pigeons perched on a beam beneath the platform began to squabble. The wind shifted, bringing a burning smell from the vats. Rosacher realized he'd become so accustomed to the dragon that most of the time he paid it no more attention than a rock—whenever he spoke about Griaule, he did so in the abstract, as if he were referring to an idea, a principle, something other than the dragon's monstrous reality.

"How's business?" Cattanay asked.

"Manageable. We make plenty of missteps, but one learns to adapt."

"It's the same with me. Always something. Loggers haven't returned with wood to keep the vats going or someone's taken a fall. I've delegated responsibility, yet it's a rare day when I'm not called away to deal with some trouble."

"At least when you're done you'll have a monument to commemorate your labors."

"The mural? I doubt it. How long do you think it'll take before they decide to rid themselves of Griaule's corpse? A week? A month? No more, surely."

Rosacher murmured in agreement.

"There's a man in Punta Esperanza who's had some success with reproducing images from life," said Cattanay. "Perhaps by the time it's finished, he'll have refined the process and the mural will survive in that way. It's hardly the same thing, though."

Cattanay had another bite of sandwich and Rosacher, kicking his heels against the side of the platform, said, "May I ask a personal question?"

His mouth full, Cattanay signaled him to go ahead.

"Are you happy?"

Cattanay swallowed, wiped his mouth. "That's a hell of a question...though I hear it often. Allie asks it of me almost every night."

"I'm certain the context is very different."

"Oh, without a doubt." Cattanay picked at a bit of food trapped between his teeth. "Happy's not a word I generally apply to myself. You might say I'm content. I'm doing work I love. Things aren't perfect, but I suppose I'm happy enough. Happier than you by the look of it."

"You'll get no argument from me on that account."

Tipping his head to the side, Cattanay seemed to study him as though he were a troublesome area on a canvas. "Perhaps you lack passion," he said. "That's what people need in order to know even a minute's happiness.

Without passion and the focus passion brings, there's only confusion. That's how I view it, anyway."

"I used to be passionate about science, but no more. I was never passionate about the business. The business...it was something to do, something easier than science. I thiink I've used it as an excuse not to do what I really wanted."

"You'd best find something else you really want, then. That is, if happiness is your goal."

"I think my goals may be changing."

"Pah! Mine change a dozen times each morning before lunch. I'll wish for a better source of a magenta and then the sight of an art student with a nice *derriere*...well, you know how it goes."

With a grunt, Cattanay got to his feet. He balled up the paper in which his sandwich had been wrapped and tossed it off the tower. Thin streams of people were passing in the streets below. "I have things to take care of at the vats. Have you been up on the dragon recently?"

"Not for years...and then only to the edge of the mouth."

Cattanay stepped into the basket of the elevator attached to the side of the tower and prepared to lower himself. "You ought to take a walk up there when you have a chance. It can be inspiring. You never know what you might encounter."

✠

After puttering in his laboratory the rest of the morning and into late afternoon, unable to come to grips with the scientific elements of the issue that confronted him, Rosacher heeded Cattanay's advice and climbed the scaffolding to the vats and then walked out onto the dragon's back, following a meandering track through dry-leaved thickets until he came to Hangtown. The settlement had grown from a handful of shacks surrounding a polluted puddle of rainwater half an acre in circumference to a village of perhaps two hundred souls housed in fifty or sixty shanties, the largest of these serving as a tavern and marked by a neatly hand-lettered sign that read:

MARTITA'S HOME IN THE SKY

It was a relatively new structure with windows that were not merely square holes in the walls, but had panes of warped, opaque glass, and its wood was still a roach-brown, not faded to gray like the majority of the shanties; yet it was equally as ramshackle, with a slumping roofed porch and a partial second floor that appeared to be in the process of sliding off. A man—a scalehunter judging by his profusion of green and gold tattoos—sprawled unconscious in a chair on the front porch, an advertisement for the effectiveness of the establishment's spirits. Having experienced neither exhilaration nor inspiration during his walk, Rosacher entered the spacious common room and its atmosphere of gloom and fried onions, thinking a pint would help fuel his descent to Morningshade. Behind the bar (boards laid across a half-dozen barrels), a robust, round-faced woman of thirty or thereabouts, unprepossessing in aspect, her brown hair in long braids, dressed in cloth breeches (a style favored by Hangtown's female population—skirts tended to catch on twigs and thorns) and a low-cut blouse, busied herself with polishing mugs. An elderly white-haired man with a scarred face and a man young enough to be his grandson played cards at a bench by the window. They eyed him indifferently and the woman came bustling over to Rosacher, who had taken a seat at the rear.

"We've a good blond ale from Port Chantay," she said. "Otherwise it's homebrew. Quite nice, it is, and very strong, if that's your pleasure."

Rosacher opted for the ale and cast an eye about the room. Basically unadorned, it had here and there a feminine touch: gillyflowers in a vase; a print showing Griaule against a mass of clouds; a framed needlepoint homily with letters so crooked that he was unable to read them. The woman returned with the ale, she hovered beside the table, and after he had paid her she continued to hover. He had a sip and said, "This will do," thinking she wanted him to approve the ale, yet she remained standing by the table, beaming at him. Finally she said, "You don't remember me, do you? Truly, there's no reason you should. You didn't take much notice of my face." She winked broadly. "You were mainly interested in my backside."

"I beg your pardon?"

"Martita." She tapped her ample bosom, dislodging a silver locket that had been half-concealed in her cleavage, the image of a dragon scratched on the casing as if by her own hand. "Martita Doans. I was a maid in your house. The night the assassin came, it were me what was sent to bandage you." She dropped her voice to a whisper. "We made love."

The term "made love" befuddled him for a moment and, once he had sorted it out, feeling embarrassed, shamed, yet not wishing to admit to anything, he said weakly, "Of course. Uh, I…How've you been?"

"Lately I've been doing very well, thank you. But directly after I left your service, now that were a bit of rough road, what with me being in a family way and having no family to turn to."

She took a seat opposite him and leaned forward, her milky breasts squashed against the tabletop, threatening to overflow their flimsy restraint. "I wanted to tell you, seeing how the babe was yours, but that Ludie hustled me out so fast I scarce had time to pack," she said in a stage whisper. "And Mr. Honeyman said if I gave him any trouble, he'd let his men at me and sell tickets to whoever cared to watch. So there I were, out on the streets and big as a house. I couldn't even sell meself." She dropped back into a normal tone. "Griaule knows what would have happened had not Mister Doans— that's my late husband, Nathan Doans—took me in."

"I had no idea!" Rosacher said. "I mean I wouldn't..."

"I didn't figure you did. Mister Honeyman made it clear I wasn't to pester you. He said that should I try to inform you of my situation, there'd be hell to pay. Still and all, I didn't think kindly toward you those first months."

The elderly card player called to her and Martita went to see what he wanted. Stunned by what he had learned, Rosacher drained his pint in two swallows. If what she told him was true, and he had no reason to doubt her, Ludie and Arthur had much to answer for. Not that he would have done much better than they for Martita. He likely would not have accepted paternity of the child, yet he would have at least seen to its care and feeding. It seemed he could feel a space inside himself that affection for a child would have occupied, and this sparked a deeper resentment. He would have to rein in Arthur and Ludie, rein them in sharply, perhaps even to the point of reconfiguring the business—they had been acting more-or-less independently in recent years, and probably not to his benefit. It might be time for a house-cleaning. Neither of them were indispensable and it was evident he could no longer trust them.

Martita returned, bringing a second pint, and he asked, "The child? Is it a boy or a girl?"

Her face fell. "It were a boy. I couldn't carry it to term."

Speechless for a moment, he said, "I obviously can't make things right, but you must let me help."

"I don't want for much. Mister Doans was a scalehunter, like most here. He did very well for himself. Found several loose scales of museum quality during his day." She shook her head ruefully. "Two years back it were he died…and him still a young man. But that's the way of it with scalehunters, ain't it?" She nodded toward the card players. "Jarvis is the only one I know what's lived past middle years. For all the good it does him. He's a miserable sod. But like I was saying, Mister Doans left me the tavern and a tidy sum besides. I've a decent life now."

"There must be something I can do."

"You might stop in and have a pint now and again. Having you here tones up the place." She blushed. "And it would please me."

"Why would you want me around? First I force myself upon you and then…"

"Oh, don't be thinking that! Maybe that was your view of things, but it weren't mine. All the girls what worked in the house had an eye for you…and me most of all."

"I see."

"I could have done with a little romance, but you heard no complaints from me at the time and you'll hear none now."

Perplexed as much by his concern for her as by her forgiving attitude, he said, "If you want me to come around, I will...though I question whether either the moral or spiritual tenor of your establishment will be improved by my presence."

She apparently didn't understand his words and simpered to cover her confusion.

"Well." She rubbed her hands together and beamed. "I need to start me cooking. Folks will be wanting their tucker."

He would have liked to catch her hand and make some promise, swear an oath to right all wrongs done her, but shame and the fear of a weakness that shame might reveal locked him into a stoic posture, for he had come to think of himself as a hard man and now, recognizing he was not, understanding how drastically he had changed during the past six years, he thought he should try to preserve the impression, at least, of rigor. He lingered a while, keeping an eye on Martita as she moved between the stove, visible through a door at the back end of the bar, and the front room, hoping business would pick up and allow him to make an inconspicuous exit. A few more customers came in, but not enough to provide him with cover. He finished his second pint, gave her a casual wave and went out.

The cool air seemed to illumine him, bringing new and untried emotions to light. He hurried past Hangtown's shallow, semi-permanent lake, filmed over by algae and scum, glazed with moonlight, realizing how isolated he had become. With Ludie leading a separate existence and Arthur spending every waking hour with the militia, his life had emptied out and, while he consorted with a variety of women and had no end of business acquaintances, he had not sought to replace these losses with relationships of an equivalent depth. In his solitude he'd had time to dwell on regrets and recriminations, and had developed a streak of self-pity; this in turn had created a sentimental side that he despised on principle, yet had come to depend on as a companion to his calculating and brutal nature, taking the place of lovers and friends. Whereas previously the sight of a mother nursing an infant or a small boy playing with a puppy would have barely registered on his consciousness, now these incidences seemed brightly human, striking him as emblematic of the world's fragility and beauty, often causing his eyes to tear. Yet he knew better than to accept this change at face value and suspected that his reactions were linked to self-interest, perhaps to a renewed apprehension of mortality and a sense that his personal failures were unredeemable.

The thickets buzzed with insignificant life, the tops of the bushes swaying in the strong wind that flowed over Griaule's back. He pushed into them, proceeding along a partly overgrown trail that led to the dragon's crest, rising like a shadowy cliff above. He had never envisioned himself with children, yet the revelation that he'd fathered a son, even one stillborn…it was as if a pebble had been dropped into the waters of his soul, one from which ripples continued to spread long after the event, and he could not cease from thinking about the lost potentials of fatherhood. Overcome by frustration, an emotion never rising to the level of grief or rage, affording him no release, he cast his eyes upward. A scatter of stars lay directly above, like a throw of cowrie shells on a fortuneteller's dark cloth, and he imagined he saw in them a blueprint for action, his life's path revealed.

"Richard!" A woman's voice at his rear.

Clad in trousers and a waist-length jacket, Ludie stood half in the spiky shadow of a century plant, considering him with a glum expression. Her presence put him on the alert—under ordinary circumstances, she would never set foot on the dragon—and he asked what she was doing there.

"Protecting my investment," she said.

Arthur moved out of the bushes to stand behind her, a long-barreled pistol dangling from his right hand. He slipped his free arm about her waist, nudging a breast with his thumb, and grinned.

"I don't know what you two have in mind," said Rosacher. "But I advise you to think things over carefully before you act."

"Oh, we done that," Arthur said. "We've thoroughly analyzed the problem, as you might say."

"Ask yourself if you're capable of running the business," Rosacher said. "You've no idea how complicated it is."

Ludie extricated herself from Arthur's grasp. "This has nothing to do with whether or not we can run the business. It has everything to do with your incompetence."

"Incompetence? Are you mad?"

"In the past year demand has outstripped supply for the first time since we began. Between theft and poor management, our profits are down nearly thirty percent from our peak...which was five years ago. You've lost your entrepreneurial instincts, Richard. Your enthusiasm for the game." She folded her arms. "We've struck a new agreement with the council. Breque has assured us he can handle day-to-day operations until we find someone to replace you."

"You're not qualified to deal with Breque," Rosacher said. "He'll have you for breakfast."

Ludie's mouth tightened.

"Why do you think he struck such a deal with you?" said Rosacher. "He knows he'll be able to outmaneuver you if I'm not around."

"I'm not an idiot. I understand that Breque will move against us."

"Understanding and doing something about it are different things. You don't have the focus, Ludie. The discipline. You won't put in eighteen hours a day when necessary. You'll be fine at first, but sooner or later you'll..."

"Arthur." She urged the giant forward with a gesture—he covered the distance between them in two steps and seized Rosacher by the collar.

"I'll meet you below," said Ludie, shooting the cuffs of her blouse. She stared at Rosacher without emotion, then turned abruptly and struck out along the path. Rosacher started to call after her, but Arthur clipped him behind the ear with the butt of his pistol and, once he had recovered from the blow, still dazed, his vision blurry, the moon jolting in and out of view, he found that Arthur was dragging him by his collar through sparse vegetation and over sloping ground, over mattes of vines, the same that partially curtained Griaule's sides. He twisted about, wanting to see where they were headed, and caught a glimpse of the lights of Teocinte spread thick as stars across the valley and recognized they were above the dragon's shoulder, very near the point where a man would have to hang onto something in order to keep from falling off the side. He flung himself about, hoping to break Arthur's grip, but to no avail, and as he cast about for some other means of escape the giant stopped and hauled him erect, holding him by the shirtfront at arm's length. Rosacher felt the chill tug of gravity and clawed at Arthur's arm, attempting to determine which tactic would be the most propitious, whether to cajole or threaten. Arthur smiled, the merest tic of a smile and said, "Mind the drop, now," and released him, simply opening his hand. Rosacher gave a terrified squawk and clutched at Arthur's sleeve. His feet skidded on the slick surface of a scale and, flailing with his arms, he managed to maintain his balance sufficiently so that he did not go somersaulting backwards off Griaule, but rather pitched forward onto his stomach and slid down the dragon's side, clutching at the edges of scales, his fingers too weak to find purchase, grabbing at vines, entangling his arm in one, more by accident than anything else, snagging another, continuing to fall, but slowly, slower yet, until he was less falling than lowering himself. To his amazement, he realized that he might not die.

The flat crack of a gunshot and a bullet ricocheted off a scale hard by Rosacher's elbow. He allowed himself to slip down beyond the curve of Griaule's ribcage, out of Arthur's sight, and hung there, doing a half-spin, bumping against a scale the size of a cathedral door, feeling terribly exposed, as might a criminal escaping prison by means of a too-short rope flung over an outer wall. To this point he had merely been reacting, but now he began to think again, albeit in a fragmented way, unmanned by the sight of Morningshade below, its flickering orange lights tiny as fireflies. The vines had been cut back from Cattanay's mural, otherwise Rosacher might have climbed across the dragon's side and then shinnied down onto the scaffolding. He could not descend to the valley floor—the longest of the vines ended hundreds of feet above the tallest rooftop—and thus he began inching across the masonry of lichen-dappled scales, moving vine-to-vine toward the shadows beneath the shoulder joint of Griaule's foreleg, planning to hide there until morning when he would climb up or, if unable to make the ascent, attract the attention of a scalehunter (areas beneath the joints were prime spots in which to find broken or loosened scales). On reaching the area he wove vines together into a makeshift seat, constructing a virtual cage of vines in which he felt relatively stable. This done, he hauled himself tight against the underside of the joint, securing the cage there, lashing it to other vines. Then and only then did he allow himself to catch his breath and take stock.

He could see nothing of his immediate surround, not even scales close enough to touch, yet it seemed that here, tucked beneath what was essentially the dragon's armpit, he could make out Griaule's scent—a pervasive cool dryness unalloyed by the lesser odors of vegetation and lichens, like that of an abandoned fortress, a mass of ancient stone tenanted by wind and the ghosts of lizards. The dragon's moonstruck side curved away like a planet armored in scales, each of considerable size save for a section about thirty feet overhead that appeared to be composed of hundreds of irregularly shaped scales four or five inches in width...or perhaps it was a single scale struck by innumerable blows that had left it cracked, divided by hundreds of fine fissures. If this were the case, the culprit would have likely been someone other than a scalehunter—scalehunters were notorious for their superstitions and their lore was rife with cautionary anecdotes concerning men who had attempted to pry loose a scale or otherwise cause the dragon to suffer a minor bodily insult, and how Griaule had exacted his revenge upon them. Rosacher was in the habit of scoffing at such stories, but now that he was more-or-less alone on the dragon, he could not dismiss them. When seen from his vantage, the beast's magnitude was no longer quantifiable. "Gargantuan" was too modest a term for a creature that was its own domain. He recalled the night he had ventured into Griaule's mouth, the army of strange insects sheltering there, the way they had moved in unison, and he understood that assigning a mystical value to the experience was not entirely irrational from a phenomenological standpoint. Thinking about Griaule as a magical figure rekindled his anxieties and, suspended by vines above a five-hundred-foot drop, staring between his feet at the lights of Morningshade, he placed his palm upon a scale and prayed to be kept safe. The prayer was tinged with shame at having surrendered to fear, yet was no less fervent for all that and, though he mentioned no names, was directed toward Griaule. Afterward he chalked it up to a weak moment, yet he felt calmer. He gazed off along the swell of the dragon's ribcage, soothed by the shimmer of moonlight on the scales, and marveled at his good fortune. Had Arthur pushed him rather than simply letting him go, he would be lying dead and broken in the street below with his every organ ruptured. He was determined to have his revenge and he needed to act swiftly, before his business was imperiled more than it already had been. Further, he would have to do something about Breque. The council had served as an effective buffer between Rosacher and the Church, a function he preferred them to continue for the foreseeable future; yet it might be the time for bold strokes. His position was not as strong as he would have liked (for one thing, he was uncertain how the militia would react if he removed Arthur as their leader; for another he had no idea what steps Breque had taken to protect himself), but he would have surprise on his side and a sufficiency of funds (salted away for just such an emergency). Within a matter of days he could hire assassins and organize their assignments; then he could sit back and orchestrate events. He'd operate out of Martita's tavern. Should things go awry, he believed he could depend on her to hide him—her dog-loyalty to him had been evident.

A faint noise interrupted the flow of his thoughts and he saw a lanky figure clambering down Griaule's side: Arthur. The giant had removed his jacket and his white silk shirt rippled with light. He had wrapped a vine about his waist, using his left hand to control his rate of descent and holding his pistol in the right. He stopped about fifty feet above and scanned the area beneath him. Holstering the pistol, he began traversing the dragon, heading in the general direction of the shoulder joint. There was nothing for Rosacher to do except pray and pray he did, initially to a nameless presence, but as Arthur drew nearer the prayers evolved into fervent pleas to Griaule, begging the dragon to distract the giant, to lead him away or cause the vine to snap. Once he had negotiated slightly more than half the distance between them, Arthur drew his pistol and fired two shots into the shadows beneath the joint, both going wide of Rosacher.

"Show yourself!" Arthur called. "I promise to end things quickly!"

Rosacher tried desperately to think of something he could do or say that might extricate him from this situation, unearthing and discarding old strategies. Suddenly he grew weary and sat plucking at the vines that constrained him. It was as if light and energy were emptying from his mind.

"If you force me to chase after you," Arthur shouted, "I promise you'll regret it!" A pause. "Do you hear?"

Rosacher suspected that Arthur might be afraid of the dark space in which he had hidden; but this did no more than give his spirits a momentary boost.

Cursing, Arthur descended a few feet and planted a boot on what Rosacher had presumed to be the shattered scale, knocking loose several of the broken pieces—against all expectation they did not fall but hovered beside Arthur, fluttering as though weightless and borne aloft on an updraft. The remainder of the pieces also fluttered up about the giant, laying bare an undamaged scale beneath. They swarmed about him like a leaf storm, almost obscuring him from sight. He screamed; his pistol discharged and he screamed a second time, his legs poking out from the mass of golden fragments that sheathed his upper body, kicking madly, presenting an image that might have been engendered by the brain of a drug-addled artist. Whatever their nature—be they insects or something more obscure—they settled on his hands, neck and face, affixing themselves to the bare skin, so that he came to resemble a man with huge golden mittens and a misshapen golden head thrice normal size that changed shape subtly, now shrinking, now growing distended. Spasms racked his body, yet he screamed no more. He hung there for a second, some reflex permitting him to maintain a grip on the vine that supported him, and then he tumbled away, spinning down against the lights of the town. The insects (Rosacher had determined they were such) came scattering back up from the falling corpse and formed into a cloud that drifted off around the curve of the dragon's ribs—once again Rosacher entertained the conceit that he was looking off along the curve of a golden planet and observing the curious astronomical object that orbited it.

Silence and stillness closed in around him and he realized he was trembling. His breath came quick and shallow, and though the night was fairly warm he felt chilled to the bone. He squeezed his eyes shut, attempting to control his body, and heard a thin keening, like a teakettle beginning to boil. Curious, he opened his eyes. An insect like those that had attacked Arthur danced before his face—a long, dark, drooping body suspended between papery gold wings. In panic, he swatted at it and it fluttered off, going out of view. He no longer heard the whining, but as he twisted about in his cage of vines, hoping to catch sight of the insect, it fluttered up from behind his back and battened onto his jaw. He made to knock it away, but did not complete the gesture—a second insect, its wings folded, perched on his middle knuckle. A sting, a pinprick attended by a cold, burning sensation, and his hand cramped, knotted into a fist. Another sting seared his neck. Cold fire spread down into his throat and across his cheek. More stings followed, how many he could not be certain. They blended into a red wash of agony, fire poison acid, a distillate of each combined to produce a fourth and commensurately greater effect. The pain had a noise, a crackling scream that he realized was issuing from his throat. He seemed to be riding atop the noise as if it were a wave, one carrying him toward a black coast that came to cast a shadow across him so deep, he could no longer distinguish movement or color or anything at all. Even his pain was subsumed, although it seemed he brought its memory with him into the blessed dark.

9

RUDDY LIGHT PRIED UNDER his eyelids and he heard somebody humming a snatch of a familiar song. A confusion of memories crowded his brain—he could make no sense of them—and a hazy figure moved across his field of vision, clarifying into a lovely Rafaelesque woman clad in breeches and a low-cut blouse. She passed into an adjoining room. He made to call out and that set off a paroxysm of coughing. Once the coughing subsided he felt dazed and out of his depth. Something partially covered his face, interfering with his breathing—he pawed at it and found that the lower half of his face and both hands were bandaged. He sank back into the mattress and wondered where he was. The room was Spartan, a few sticks of furniture, an oil lamp, unadorned walls of newly cut boards, a window covered by an orange shade—yet it had a pleasing aesthetic and the blond color of the unfinished wood glowed with a raw vitality. The bed was not much larger than a cot, though comfortable. As he grew increasingly alert he felt pain in the areas that were bandaged and called out again, cautiously this time, producing a feeble grating noise that initiated another bout of coughing. There was no response, but several minutes later the woman re-entered and he attracted her notice with a hand signal. She sat on the edge of the bed and laid a hand on his forehead, peering at him with a worried look. She asked if he needed anything and he shaped the word "water" with his lips.

After he had drunk and swallowed the medication she pressed upon him, two pastilles, he took her measure. She might be Martita's twin, he thought. They were identical in nearly every respect, yet the physical characteristics that made Martita ordinary somehow combined in this woman to effect a regal and voluptuous beauty. She leaned toward him, adjusting the pillows beneath his head, and a silver locket incised with the crude image of a dragon dangled in his face.

"Martita?" Speaking her name set off yet another spell of coughing.

"There, now!" She shushed him, putting a finger to his lips. "You'll be talking soon enough. I know you have questions, though, so I'll tell you what I can."

He nodded.

"You run afoul of a swarm of flakes, you and Mister Honeyman," she said. "You won't find as many of them this side of Griaule, the Teocinte side, as once there was. Cattanay's crew crawling all over keeps them away. Flakes likes their solitude. But now and then a swarm drifts over this way and does some damage. You only had a few stings. Most of 'em spent their poison on Mister Honeyman, I reckon. People say they had trouble identifying his remains, he were so disfigured. 'Course the fall didn't help matters none. Come right through the roof of a bathhouse, he did. Some of the ladies from Ali's Eternal Reward were lying about, taking their ease with one another, if you catch my meaning, and what with Mister Honeyman bursting in on 'em like that... well, it dimmed their mood, let's say."

Rosacher was greatly relieved by this, understanding from this that he had not lost more years, merely days.

Martita looked up into a corner of the room as if receiving intelligence from that quarter. "That woman," she went on. "Ludie. She were up here looking for you. Her and some of the militia. She said she's worried about you, but I never trusted that one, so when Jarvis found you hanging off Griaule's side, I figured to let you decide about things. If you want me to let her know you're here, I can..."

Rosacher clutched her arm and shook his head, signaling "no" in as emphatic a way as he could manage.

"I thought as much. She pretended she were desperate afraid for you, but what I took from her manner was she wanted to make sure you were dead." She patted his hand. "Don't you worry. You're safe here."

He was not so confident about this as she appeared to be, but neither was he inclined to debate the point. Weariness overtook him and, if the conversation continued for longer than that snippet, he could not later recall it.

For the better part of a week Rosacher was in and out of consciousness. One state came to resemble the other. His sleep was littered with vivid dreams that were extraordinary in nature—in them, dressed in a black hat and coat, he traveled throughout the Carbonales Valley, often to different portions of the dragon's body, even visiting Griaule's internal regions, and there he would speak with various and sundry (he could not recall much detail from these conversations, but had the impression they were significant). By contrast, his waking periods were drowsy and muddle-headed, enlivened by the stirrings of arousal he felt whenever Martita visited him. He recognized she must be giving him mab to treat his pain and this accounted for her newfound allure; but knowing that did nothing to diminish that allure. Though thicker and less dainty than the women he was accustomed to having in his bed, he did not find this off-putting. She seemed epic in dimension and he pictured her image carved bare-breasted and forward-looking on a ship's bow, or sculpted in battle dress at the head of an army, and imagined himself lifting away her bronze breastplates and pressing his lips to the bounty beneath. Toward the end of the week, when she came to clear away the remains of his supper, he pulled her close, fondled her and nuzzled her neck. She allowed him a free hand for several seconds and then went to the door and called downstairs to her assistant, Anthony, telling him to tend to the counter. When she removed her clothing, her skin gleamed as if a sun were embedded in all that whiteness. He understood that what he saw now differed from how he had once perceived her, yet he did not question his response to her and soon was lost in the soft turns of her body. She straddled him, her hands braced on his shoulders, her braids lashing his chest. Through lidded eyes he observed the quaking round of her belly, immense, pendulous breasts shaped like summer squash jouncing together, slack features pinked from exertion, these sights orchestrated by the rhythmic slapping of flesh—she seemed a divine animal in human form and he gave himself over to the act, drowning in her, devoted to her pleasure as he had been with no woman before. Afterward, lying torpid amid the rumpled bedding, he watched her buttoning her trousers and realized that, while he did not feel love toward her (he doubted he would ever know that emotion), he had no sense of disdain such as customarily attended his liaisons with unimportant women. Instead, he had an urge to make a joke or be playful in some way, but he was uncertain of his instincts in this regard and kept quiet.

"If you're strong enough to give me a bounce..." Martita cinched her belt. "You'll soon be wanting to get up and about."

She went to a closet, took out a black suit and a slouch hat, and laid them on the foot of the bed.

"Try these on when you've a mind," she said. "Mister Doans wore that suit whenever he went to town. It can take a bit of letting out if needs be."

Rosacher tried to pull her down onto the bed again, but she fended him off, saying she had to get back to the bar or else Anthony would rob her blind.

"I'll look in on you again this evening," she said. "Get some rest and we'll see how you're feeling then."

After she had left he examined Mr. Doans' suit and hat—they were identical to those he had worn in his dreams, and identical also to those worn by the man with the horrible cough and the bandaged face who had come to him in a dream on the night the Church's assassin had invaded his bedroom. He knew what Martita would say were he to bring the subject up. She'd tell him that Griaule's ways were too subtle for men to comprehend and would advise him not to waste time on matters that were beyond him. The usual drivel. And yet, he told himself, although he had backslid from this viewpoint on several prior occasions, the usual drivel was becoming ever more difficult to discount.

10

IS SCARS WERE PERMANENT and they were not the kind of scars that lent an exotic accent to a man's features. The skin covering the left side of his jaw and neck had been rendered reddish brown and displayed a coarse, rippled look, as with overdone bacon, and the backs of his hands were much the same, although the effect was not so pronounced. On discovering that the majority of Martita's patrons bore such scars, he became less self-conscious, yet nonetheless he wore high collars and often gloves, and was prone to incline his head to the left in an attempt to hide the worst of the scarring. A lingering ague caused by the flakes' poison left him weakened, and he decided to wait until he regained his strength to avenge himself upon Ludie. In truth, vengeance was no longer his first priority. During his recuperation he came to recognize that sooner or later he would have to deal with Ludie and Breque, though not to square accounts—he could live without retribution. His survival was the important thing and if sparing them was less risky than killing them, then that was the course he would choose. He doubted, however, that this would prove to be the case.

He woke each morning with the intention of cutting short his usage of mab, but when Martita brought him the pastilles he swallowed them without hesitation—he was insufficiently motivated to quit taking the drug. Five weeks had elapsed since Arthur's attempt to kill him and he couldn't recall ever having been more content. He enjoyed the rough, comfortable atmosphere of the tavern, and liked the way he felt about Martita, and he wanted to do nothing that might affect those relationships, at least until he had time to assess this situation more fully. What did it matter if his contentment were the product of chemicals? Under normal circumstances was not happiness inducd by a temporary imbalance of one kind or another? But by far the most compelling reason for using mab was that he no longer dreaded falling asleep—in addition to its palliative benefits, he had stopped losing years and, while he could not be certain that this state of affairs would continue, or that mab was the critical variable involved (it might be, he reasoned, that his sense of lost years was due to some mental affliction, now passed), he was reluctant to change any of his behaviors for fear of a relapse.

He took to helping out in the tavern, working behind the counter during the days—this allowed Martita to leave him in charge and keep the place open whenever she had business in Teocinte. In the afternoons, with the sun slanting through the windows, gilding the rough planking, the patrons encased in distinct beams of light, dust motes whirling above their heads, the kinetic representation of their illuminated thoughts, the smell of cooked apples (dragon apples, grown in a stunted orchard sprouting from Griaule's back, valued for their medicinal properties), all the peace and sweetness of the place…it was so quiet, so quaint and homey, so unlike any environment Rosacher had known, it charmed him and he basked in that charm, in that ruddy, glowing space, recognizing it for an illusion, knowing that people could ruin any such space with their bloody-minded urges, yet embracing the illusion for as long as it would last. Not long, as it turned out. Before two months had passed, the confines of his new life, giving Martita a daily bounce and having superficial, simpleminded (for the most part) chats with the patrons and handling the ordinary business of the tavern…they began to chafe at him. Mab prevented the chafing from growing too pronounced— it manifested as a nagging sense of dissatisfaction that he could have easily ignored; but Rosacher was not a man who overlooked imperfections and he picked away at this mental sore each day until the only thing that would reduce the aggravation was another pastille.

While talking one afternoon with Jarvis Riggins, the elderly scalehunter who had rescued him from beneath the dragon's shoulder, Rosacher expressed this very dissatisfaction. Jarvis wore his usual costume of leather trousers and a sleeveless canvas shirt; his arms, cheek, and neck were festooned with tattoos, the majority being tiny representations of green-and-gold scales that signified important finds. The largest of his tattoos was all but hidden by his shirt, a dragon rampant, a portion of the head showing above his collar. He sat facing away from the window, his cloudy nimbus of white hair backlit by the late sun into a flaming halo, his scarred, crumpled face in shadow, a visage so ruinous it might have been an element of terrain that, when seen from a great elevation, resembled a human caricature. He inquired if Rosacher knew where he was and, without waiting for an answer to his question, asked another: "Do they have herds of mile-long dragons where you come from, boy? They must...else how can you live here and not realize you're walking around on top of a miracle?"

Rosacher let out an exasperated sigh. "I've had a bellyful of that nonsense. Griaule knows. Griaule will provide. Griaule will answer all of your prayers."

Jarvis scraped at a tattooed scale on his wrist with a fingernail. "He answered your prayer, didn't he?"

"I'm sorry I told you about that," Rosacher said. "It's true. I've had moments when I've allowed fear to get the best of me. When I've been tempted to cling to superstition. But when I look at the world with a rational eye, I see nothing that will not one day be subject to a clear and credible scientific explanation."

Jarvis grunted. "It's like I said. You don't know where you are."

"Well." Rosacher swiped at moisture on the counter with a rag. "If Griaule's a god, he's a wildly erratic one. His actions seem completely random."

The old man made as if to speak, but Rosacher beat him to the mark: "And I don't want to hear any talk of his inscrutable purposes, his mysterious ways. I've had a bellyful of that, too."

A customer in the back hailed Rosacher and he went to fetch him another pint. The sun shone straight in through the windows of the tavern and the scattering of solitary figures sitting at benches and along the counter with their heads lowered to their mugs resembled figures in a monastic setting, meditating upon some subtle doctrinal issue, encased in beams of dusty light that enriched the reddish color of the boards. Rosacher responded to a second summons and, by the time he returned to his spot by the window, Jarvis was preparing to leave.

"I'll stop back tomorrow at first light," said the old man. "I want to take you out under the wing, show you something."

"What is it?"

"You can decide that for yourself. Bring food and water for the day."

Rosacher protested that he might have to work and Jarvis said, "Martita's been running this place alone since Nathan died. She can manage for a day."

"Isn't there some animal living under the wing that's supposed to be dangerous?"

"It won't bother us none as long as we don't go in too deep...and I ain't even sure it's still there. Been a while since it did for anyone."

"What about flakes? If all you're suggesting is a nature walk, I have no desire to be stung again."

"Flakes won't bother you no more. Once they sting you, they're done. You could walk into the midst of a swarm and they'd pay you no mind."

Unable to think of a reasonable explanation for such behavior, one that would accord with the imperatives of biological necessity, Rosacher asked why this was.

"Mysterious ways," Jarvis said.

✠

AT DAWN THE next day, with a shimmering red sun balanced in a notch between distant hills, Jarvis and Rosacher (burdened by two twelve-foot-long bamboo poles that Jarvis had cut along the way, to the ends of which he had affixed large hooks, offering no explanation other than "...they'll come in handy...") lowered themselves on ropes to a spot beneath the dragon's wing where an ancient wound—a wedge torn from the flesh over which the scales had grown back warped and deformed—had evolved over millennia into a wide ledge that afforded a view of Griaule's eastern slope and the countryside below. The scales on that side were obscured by tangles of vines and carpeted in lichen that ranged in hue through a spectrum of vivid greens, with here and there edgings of rust and scarlet and pale brown. Dirt and grass mounded high beneath the dragon's belly, covering much of his legs, making it appear from a westbound traveler's perspective that this portion of the beast was a natural formation, a cliff lifting from a plain of palms and thorn bushes and tall yellow grasses. Only the wing, drooping down to shade the ledge, scarcely ten feet overhead, its great vanes and struts supporting a considerable acreage of darkly veined tissue, denied this impression. As the sun climbed higher, the sky lightening to a robin's egg blue with pink streamers of cloud feathered above the hills, it brought to light the abundance of life that flourished upon and about Griaule. Swarms of insects darted to and fro, doing some dervish duty, and occasionally a cloud of flakes drifted into view, causing Rosacher to tense until they passed from sight. Uncountable thousands of creatures too small to make out moved across Griaule's body, creating a rippling effect, as if he were seeing through a depth of crystalline water. Hawks patrolled the skies, swooping down to take their prey, and flocks of smaller birds—swifts, starlings, sparrows, and so forth—swept up and away, or flew low above the dragon, following the topography of the back for a second or two before vanishing in the direction of Teocinte. The organic complexity of the scene put him in mind of childhood summers spent on the coast, diving down into the translucent water and observing the reef, the strange unity of fishes darting in schools beneath the shadows of sharks, gorgonians and anemones gently waving, many-jointed crustaceans, frail life forms whose curious configurations beggared classification, a myriad trivial interactions joined in a symphony of movement that seemed to reflect the direction of an enormous brain, to be its living thoughts.

After half an hour Jarvis turned onto his side and went to sleep, leaving Rosacher to contemplate the vista without the benefit of the old man's minimalist conversation…and that, Rosacher assumed, was the point of the exercise: to make him aware of the biotope that Griaule had become, supporting a vast biotic community; to have him experience it and be amazed and let him mistake it for divinity. Well, he was amazed, the view was spectacular; but he perceived in the centrality of Griaule to the biocoenosis not proof of divinity, but rather evidence of the principles expressed by men of science such as Alfred Russell Wallace and Alexander Von Humboldt. And so, armored against magical thinking and superstition in all its guises, he leaned back against a scale and gazed at the dragon's wing, suspended above like a remnant of a huge broken umbrella. A variety of birds—wrens, orioles, grackles, caciques, and the like—had suspended their nests along the underside of the wing, some of them quite elaborate, and the air was busy with their flights. Hundreds of them perched along the wing's edge preparatory to soaring up and away in their search for food, and Rosacher became mesmerized in tracking their dartings and swoopings. As he watched his thoughts moved in similarly erratic orbits, passing from topic to topic without apparent logical connection until he found himself considering his business in relation to Griaule, noting mistakes and missed opportunities. Prominent among these was the idea that things would have gone much easier if, instead of scoffing at those who professed belief in Griaule's divinity, he had embraced them, if he had promoted mab as the sacrament of a living god and held up addiction as an exemplar of religious faith. Why, he wondered, had he not seen this before? Had he done so, there was no telling how far his influence might have spread, how powerful he would have become. Neither the Church in Mospiel, nor any church, for that matter, could stand against a religion that delivered on its promises in the here and now, whose sacrament bestowed rewards that were tangible and immediate, and not some vague post-mortem fantasy. There would have been difficulties—the Church would have been loathe to yield up its power, yet yield it they would have. Given that the faith of their devotees could be subverted by the swallowing of a pastille, how could they not?

As he imagined the world he could have made, picturing himself ruling over the length and breadth of the littoral, perhaps over an even more substantial realm, he recalled staring out a window in his apartment at the lights of Morningshade many years before and seeing in their patterns an answer to his problems so flawlessly simple as to seem the product of a visitation. His current problems were not as severe, but the solution he had extracted from (or had been offered by) the patterns of the birds was, he realized, no less elegant, no less mysterious in its advent...and, he told himself, no less relevant. This was not a missed opportunity. He could still take advantage of it. In fact, it might be easier now that he would only have to deal with a single person: Breque. Ludie would be assiduous in her attention to detail for a while, but gradually she would cede her authority to Breque and give herself over to the pursuit of pleasure. By the time Rosacher was ready to move against Breque, her role would likely be reduced to that of a figurehead.

Of course he might not have to move against Breque; he might be able to turn him into a complicitor—that was something he would have to explore, but first things first. He needed a building, an edifice the equal of a

LUCIUS SHEPARD

cathedral and devoted to a similar purpose, yet constructed in such a fashion so that its function would be unclear to the Church until late in the day. Not that their knowledge of his plans would make a difference one way or another. They would rattle their sabers and might, in extremis, be provoked to send an army against Teocinte; but the militia had grown powerful enough to defend the city and, once Mospiel's troops had a taste of mab, it would be a short war.

Movement caught his eye—something crawling toward them about fifty feet below their perch. Not crawling, exactly. It appeared to be oozing toward them, inching along. He couldn't make out the particulars of the shape, but it seemed quite large, seven or eight feet wide, and flattish, a motley green in color (or else it was covered in lichen). Every so often it lifted what Rosacher supposed to be its head, exposing a ridge of liverish flesh marked by dark round splotches. He thought about waking Jarvis, but no threat being imminent (the creature's pace was glacial), he resolved to keep an eye on it and let the old man sleep. Two longish wires (feelers, he realized) poked up in the interstitial area between two scales adjoining his, distracting him. The insect or whatever-it-was never showed itself, however, and he fell into a drowsy reverie, making idle lists of things he would do if he intended to put his plan into action...and was jolted awake by a blow to his leg and Jarvis yelling at him to lend a hand.

The creature had closed to within six feet, lifting itself off the scale, revealing more of its liverish underside, including a lipless slash that Rosacher assumed to be a mouth. It waggled and rippled like the tip of a dark tongue, and emitted glutinous grunts as if its mouth were full of mush. Jarvis fended it off with one of the poles, jabbing at the dark splotches with the hook—they weren't discolorations, but furred bulges. Rosacher grabbed the second pole and began jabbing as well. The creature's strength nearly knocked him down, but he persevered and, after several minutes of strenuous effort, they succeeded in diminishing the thing's enthusiasm for the fight. It lowered its head and retreated, backing away, following the same track it had used in its approach.

Jarvis, leaning on his pole, said between gasping breaths, "Haven't seen one of them for ages. Thought they'd died out."

"What in the hell was it?"

"Devil's tongue. Amarga lengua. Folks had lots of names for them. They'll sneak up on you and numb you with poison. Then they'll ooze all on top of you, cover you like a shroud, and when they leave, won't be nothing left of you, not even a stain." Jarvis grinned and brandished his pole. "Told you these would come in handy."

"Is that why you brought them?" Rosacher asked, incredulous. "But how could you have known? You said you hadn't seen a...a Devil's tongue for years."

"No, that's not why!" Jarvis pointed up at the wing. "I thought we might take down a few nests. The tourists loves them. They'll pay right handsomely for the fancy ones."

11

HIS INCIDENT MARKED FOR Rosacher the beginning of his conversion, although an observer might have said it had begun long before. It was a subtle process, a gradual ascension into a state of faith, of unquestioning belief. Over the next several years (years actually lived, not skipped over and half-remembered), as he constructed the foundations of his religion and the temple that would house it, he could not put from his mind the serenity of the view from Griaule's eastern side. Time and again he visited the ledge where he and Jarvis had stationed themselves and let that serenity pervade and inspire him, filling his head with odd thoughts and insights that would drift about in his brain for days or weeks until it became clear how they applied to some issue at hand.

The greater part of these insights consisted of refinements to the design of the religion and the temple...which was disguised as that most typical of Morningshade businesses: a brothel, one that opened its doors three years before the building had been completed. Rosacher saw no reason why fleshly pleasures could not be used to enhance the ecstasies of religion—it would, to his way of thinking, only create a stronger bond between celebrant and an objectified god. He recruited women (and a goodly number of men) not from Teocinte, but from towns along the coast, the only requisites being that they were beautiful and willing to learn the scripts he wrote for them. He didn't worry whether or not they were dependable sorts, knowing that an addiction to mab would sublimate their wilder impulses and cause them to believe in the words they spoke to the patrons. Using the funds he had secreted, a massive sum, and operating through proxies, he bought the Hotel Sin Salida, then tore it down and intiated the construction of a much larger and more splendid establishment, the House of Griaule. When finished (the House, as it came to be known), resembled half an eleven-tiered wedding cake buttressed by the dragon's ankle and foreleg, and topped by twin spires, its shape reminiscent of a gothic cathedral. Yet the building's various conceits—ornate trims, Asiatic accents done in garish colors, a profusion of lanterns encased in ruby glass, hundreds of carved wooden dragons coated in gilt placed here and there about the façade—detracted considerably from this impression. Thus the immediate effect was of an immense bawdy house, while the subliminal effect was of a house of worship, which was precisely Rosacher's intent.

The four bottom floors were of granite block quarried in the hills surrounding the Carbonales Valley and contained offices, dressing rooms (patrons were required to wear robes of white linen), an extensive kitchen, banquet rooms, security rooms in which miscreants were dealt with by a highly efficient force, storerooms where stocks of wine, viands and mab were kept, etc...but the majority of the space was occupied by a vast amphitheater furnished with sofas and chaise lounges into which patrons were ushered and there welcomed by beautiful women in white silk robes and men in silk trousers, all emblazoned with the image of a golden dragon coiled around a miniature sun. The function of this space was to introduce patrons to the variety of pleasures and pleasure-givers available to them, but it was also here that their conversion began. At the bottom of the amphitheater lay a stage dominated by a marble-and-gold bas relief of Griaule beneath which dancers clad in gauzy costumes performed erotic ballets to the tune of a small orchestra (strings, flutes, French horns, and guitars), a soft music audible throughout the enclosure, yet due to the acoustic perfection of the space, this in no way impeded the conversations between patrons and the men and women of the House. These conversations were, of course, flirtations that led inevitably to sexual activity in one or another of the rooms above the fourth floor, but into each the ministrants injected portions of the homilies that Rosacher had written for them, ruminations on Griaule's nature, paeans to his magnificence and so forth...and this strategem (for such it was) continued to be used in the bedchambers, where every sexual act, however deviant, was preceded by a prayer to an image of Griaule mounted above the headboard.

Rosacher's idea was to create a fantasy religion that wedded the sybaritic to a faux-spirituality, one that skirted the edge of sacrilege and would eventually transition to the status of a "real" religion. Since the population of the Carbonales already half-believed in Griaule's divinity, it took little persuasion to push them over the brink of faith—yet even tourists having no familiarity with Griaule or mab came away from the House wearing souvenir dragon necklaces or bracelets embedded with pieces of scale (sold in the gift shop) that they were prone to touch during stressful moments, and their speech was peppered with catchphrases and fragments of litany that had been whispered in their ears during their stay. Seeing how easily people surrendered their wills to the embrace of his scheme, Rosacher envisioned Teocinte as a mecca to which pilgrims from Houses of Griaule spread around the world would flock to celebrate their god; but that was a dream that would only come to fruition if he succeeded in negotiating the hazards that confronted him.

Early in the proceedings, when the top three floors were still unfinished, but the House was already open for business, a functionary of the Church, a cardinal sent from Mospiel, visited the offices and asked to speak with the person in charge. Instead of steering him to one of Rosacher's proxies, a young office worker, knowing no better, escorted him into the fourth floor laboratory, a windowless room whose walls of unfinished stone resembled those of a prison, where Rosacher (working in the House psuedonymously) was engaged in his study of Griaule's blood. The cardinal was a fleshy man with an aquiline nose and thick gray hair and the beginnings of a double chin, wearing on his ring finger a huge gemstone of the sort set above the cathedral atop Haver's Roost, and clad in a black robe trimmed with silver. He wandered about for a time without acknowledging Rosacher, his gaze lingering on the vials and alembics and other scientific apparati that cluttered the several countertops. Only after completing his inspection did he address Rosacher, who had hovered all the while. He first surveyed Rosacher, taking in his shabby clothing, the scarring on his face and hands, and then with a haughty air, said, "I asked to speak with the person in charge."

"You're after seeing Mister Mountroyal, I reckon," said Rosacher, affecting a country àccent. "He's not here. You'll have to speak to me or one of the other administrators."

"I'll wait," the cardinal said. "I would like to meet with him today, but tomorrow in the morning will do."

"I don't suppose I made myself clear. Mister Mountroyal lives across the water on Saint Cecilia's Isle. Take him the best part of a week for to get here. Longer if he's occupied elsewhere."

The cardinal let out a petulant sigh. "If I must wait, I will wait. Prepare accommodations for me and my assistant."

"Perhaps..." Rosacher pretended to falter, to be ill at ease. "Perhaps Your Eminence should consider finding more suitable quarters. The rectory on Haver's Roost, for instance."

"I've dwelled among the sinful all my life," the cardinal said pompously, as if this were a unique accomplishment. "Nothing that occurs here will have the slightest effect upon me."

We'll have to see about that, Rosacher said to himself. He went to the wall and pulled on a bell rope. Momentarily another office worker appeared and Rosacher instructed him to ready two rooms, and to make certain anything that the cardinal might find offensive was removed.

"No, no! I am here to observe the normal functioning of your establishment. Leave everything in place." The cardinal spotted a wooden chair in the corner, went to it and settled himself, spreading his robes beneath him as might a woman. "I wish you to convey a message to your Mister Mountroyal," he said, addressing himself to Rosacher. "Tell him Cardinal Chiano has come from

Mospiel to question him about the objectionable tone of his business. I will not leave until I have met with him. Can you manage that?"

"I can." Rosacher walked to the door, but paused with his hand on the knob. "Would Your Eminence mind if I asked a question?"

Chiano gave a nearly imperceptible nod.

"What did you mean by 'objectionable tone?'"

"Surely it's obvious. In every aspect of your business, you appear to be mocking the Church."

Rosacher feigned amazement. "Why, that's not so. If anything, we're mocking the folks who think Griaule is divine."

"Griaule may well be divine. The council appointed by the Church has not yet made its determination."

"Well sir, I'm sure there are wiser heads on your council than me, but I've lived close by Griaule my entire life and I'm here to tell you, that pile of stink behind us ain't nothing more than a half-dead lizard. A whopping big lizard, but a lizard all the same."

"What makes you so certain?"

"If Griaule was a god, you think he would have let us drill into his hide so as to stabilize the biggest whore-house in the country?"

"You actually drilled into the beast?"

"Mister Mountroyal figured what with the size of the place, we couldn't rely on cables like the old hotel that stood here did."

Chiano pursed his lips. "You may have a point."

"People in these parts are crazy for religion. We didn't have the Church until recently, so folks worshipped what there was to worship. If Griaule wasn't around, you could stick an empty wine bottle up on a rock and someone would say a prayer to it. When you get right down to it, the House is doing the Church's work by associating the lizard with, if you'll pardon my language, a nice piece of fish. It causes folks to see their superstitious nonsense in a new light."

"It's an interesting point of view, I'll hand you that," said Chiano. "What's your name?"

"Myree," said Rosacher, suspecting that he had said too much and thus sparked the prelate's interest in him. "Arthur Myree."

"Well, Arthur, perhaps we'll have the opportunity to chat again."

As Rosacher made to leave, the cardinal waved at the countertops and asked what was the purpose of all this equipment.

"It's Mister Mountroyal's hobby. Ever fooling around with chemicals, he is. He taught me a few tricks and when I have a spare minute or two, I like to come in here and fiddle."

Rosacher excused himself and, once alone in his office, seated at his desk, he pondered the problem that the cardinal presented. Not that the problem was severe. Over the years he had discovered that the Church's state of decay was greater than he had assumed and he doubted they had a taste for a military engagement with a militia very nearly the equivalent of their own—there were other areas into which they could expand with little or no resistance. They might make a show of force and send more fat-assed emissaries to admonish and threaten, but as Rosacher read the situation, that was all they would do. Still, the cardinal's presence posed an opportunity for Rosacher to strengthen his position. It would take less than a day to prepare the actor who played the fictitious Mr. Mountroyal to deal with Chiano, but Rosacher intended to delay the cardinal's departure as long as he reasonably could, the better to explore the possibilities. After thinking the matter through, he summoned the office worker who had shown the cardinal into his laboratory.

"I believe Mister Mountroyal told you never to bring visitors to me," Rosacher said. "Some people find my disfigurement off-putting."

"Sorry, sir," said the office worker, who was still in his twenties and already bald on top except for a smattering of pale red strands combed across his scalp. "I was flustered. I've never been so close to a cardinal before."

"And how did you find it?"

"Beg pardon, sir?"

"Being so close to him. Was it thrilling? Did it cause you to feel faint? Did it have a transfiguring effect? Has your faith in the Church been restored?"

"Oh...no, sir."

"Something must have triggered your reaction."

"I suppose..."

"Yes?"

"The size of his ring, sir. The stone. I suppose that was what did it."

"Nothing else influenced you. No other impressions?"

"Well, sir, the main thing I noticed he breathed heavy when he walked...and he had a most peculiar body odor."

"The odor of saintliness, no doubt," said Rosacher. He slapped his desk, a decisive gesture. "All right. Try not to let it happen again. Now..." He leaned back and put his feet up on the desk. "I want you to see to Cardinal Chiano's needs. Keep a record of everything he orders from the kitchen, what he drinks, and how he passes his time. If you do a good job, I won't report your error in protocol to Mister Mountroyal."

"Thank you, sir. I'll do my best."

"One thing more. I want you to assign our most attractive available male escort to be the cardinal's personal servant for the duration of his stay."

"A man, sir?"

"It's just a feeling I have," Rossacher said.

✚

DURING THE CONSTRUCTION of the House and for several years thereafter, a period in which the business of the place began the transition from prostitution to actual religion, Rosacher maintained his living arrangement in Hangtown with Martita; but as time passed he spent more and more time away from home. Though he still found Martita attractive—and how could he not?—he did not love her, nor she him. While mab was a great leveler, all but eliminating jealousy among its users (why should one covet another wonan, a bigger house, finer clothes, when one already possessed perfection?), it could not counterfeit or induce strong emotion. And thus, the bonds of infatuation having weakened, Rosacher and Martita took other lovers, yet continued to cohabit on an intermittent basis and remained great friends.

One morning, as Rosacher prepared to walk out to the ledge to contemplate and perhaps find a solution to a pressing problem, he stood before the mirror, adjusting his hat so that it shadowed his ravaged face, a habit he rarely shirked, even in Hangtown where such injuries were common...on that morning, then, Martita came to stand at his shoulder and said in a glum voice, "You know, you haven't changed a bit since you got here."

He laughed, gesturing at his scarred cheek and neck. "You're not serious?"

"Aside from that, you look the same as you did the day you walked in. What's it been? Nearly ten years? And here's me, turning into an old woman."

He offered reassurances about her looks and, after she had gone off to pack him a lunch, he examined himself in the mirror. The scars made it difficult to judge, but it seemed to him that the unaffected area of his face was relatively unlined and his hair did not appear to be appreciably greyer. Odd. He imagined that the lack of stress had much to do with it. The drug business had been nerve-wracking, whereas the construction and organization of the House was something he looked forward to each and every day, difficult, but a joyful challenge, and not in the least stressful. At the end of a working day he would be tired, but not on edge, unable to sleep, his mind occupied with paranoid fantasies, some of which proved not to be fantasies.

He strode along Griaule's western slope to reach the ledge and on glancing down he saw, stretching out from the southern perineter of Morningshade, a plain upon which infantry and mounted troops rushed back and forth, raising clouds of whitish dust that curtained the air. The militia making ready for a sortie against the neighboring country of Temalagua (a dangerous course, in Rosacher's view), a reprisal for what had been countenanced as "Temalaguan aggression." The incident in question involved a hunting party from Teocinte that had strayed across the border and been slaughtered by the primitives who lived in the rain forest—it was generally viewed as an excuse for the council, now entirely controlled by Breque, to initiate a conflict that would result in the annexation of Temalagua's northern province, long the subject of dispute between the two governments. The fact that the province was rich in minerals and had a thriving seaport with a much deeper draft than that of Port Chantay was, of course, merely a coincidence. He stood watching the ugly chaos of the scene for a moment, wondering if he would have to intervene and listening to the disharmonious noises issuing from below, faint hammerings and crashes, and then went on his way.

The wind kicked up, clouds with dark swollen bellies rushed in from the east, and a few drops fell. Rosacher hurried along, arriving at the ledge scant minutes before the drizzle turned into a torrential downpour, drumming on the wing overhead and driving the birds to roost. Instead of addressing his problems, he let the sound of the rain lull him to sleep. When he woke, the overcast still held above Griaule, but there was a sunbreak to the east, a beam of light spraying down like a ray focused through a gigantic crystal, as if God or someone were using a magnifying glass to incinerate a portion of the coast. Birds flew out from their nests, testing the air, then returning to squabble briefly before flying off in search of breakfast. Water dripped from the cartilaginous edges of the wing. The whole of creation seemed to have been renewed by the rain—things crawled, scuttled, hopped and soared, creating the impression of organic unity that so fascinated Rosacher, that he had come to prize, even to depend on for its soothing effect. And he wondered, not for the first time, at the clear duality posed by the view from this side of the dragon and the sheer gracelessness visible from the western slope, the former being, he assumed, the idyllic albeit savage world of Griaule's origins, and the latter representing the world into which he had been thrust, a savage place also, but betraying no sign of tranquility or unified function, reflecting the erratic, the inconsistent, the poisonous delirium predicated by the human contaminant. Yet was not Griaule in part responsible for that delirium? Rosacher had spent his formative years in a Prussian village, his university days in Berlin—both places had seemed orderly and firmly regulated. The dysfunctional condition of Teocinte and environs might be the product of a torment visited upon it by Griaule. Or perhaps Prussia was not as orderly as he recalled. He decided that he would have to travel more widely and observe other cultures before reaching a conclusion.

His mind continued to run this course for a time, pushing about the notion of Griaule's duality, and he was considering whether or not to write something on the subject in order to organize his thoughts when a man's voice hailed him. Looking behind him, Rosacher saw two men standing atop the dragon's ridged spine, one holding a long-barreled rifle. The shorter of the men waved and began scrambling down

LUCIUS SHEPARD

the slope toward him; the other shouldered his rifle and remained in place. As the man drew near, Rosacher recognized him to be Councilman Breque, a much greyer version of the Breque he first met. He came up to a knee, suddenly wary, casting about for an escape route. When Breque reached the ledge, he stood for a moment with hands on hips, catching his breath and gazing out over the valley.

"Lovely spot," he said. "A touch precipitous for my taste, but it's truly spectacular." He pointed to a section of scale beside Rosacher. "Do you mind?"

"Don't see no sign stopping you," said Rosacher, affecting his country accent.

Breque lowered himself and, after he was settled, said. "It's been a long time, hasn't it?"

"Beg pardon?"

"A long time since we've spoken. It must be nearly a decade."

Rosacher scratched behind his ear. "I don't reckon I understand what you're getting at."

Breque's mouth twitched, as if he were suppressing a smile. "I know who you are, Richard. You can drop that ridiculous accent."

Rosacher kept silent, thinking that he could bolt deeper in under the wing and perhaps elude pursuit among the folds.

"If you believe I'm here to harm you," Breque went on, "let me assure you that is scarcely the case."

"It might be more persuasive if your man were to put his rifle down."

"Don't concern yourself with him. He's here to safeguard me, not to menace you."

"A fine distinction, that," said Rosacher. "Since one seems a corollary to the other."

Breque gave an exasperated sigh. "I've known where you were for almost the entire time you've been *missing*. Mister Honeyman's death and the absence of a body to counterfeit your own...I always suspected you were alive, though Ludie insisted otherwise. I think it was wishful thinking on her part and, once I found you, I saw no reason to disabuse her of her belief. Anyway, I've been keeping an eye on you all these years."

A freshet of rain pattered on the scales, diminishing almost instantly to a sprinkle.

"For what purpose?" Rosacher asked.

"You're a clever man, Richard. That's reason enough. Who can say to what ends your cleverness might be directed?"

"I have no plans to move against you. I wish to be left to my own devices. Nothing more."

"Well and good," said Breque. "I'm relieved to hear you bear me no malice. But the point I'm making is this—if I had wanted you murdered, I've had ample opportunity to accomplish that goal. I consider you a valuable resource. In fact, I have treated you as such in your absence from the business and continued to pay a percentage of our profits into your accounts. And I have allowed you to siphon off however much product you required for the functioning of the House."

Startled by this, Rosacher managed to maintain a neutral expression. "I purchase mab from…"

"From the Bornish Brothers in Port Chantay. You pay less than cost, a token amount, because the Bornish Brothers Trading House is owned by you…or rather by your proxy, Samuel Mountroyal."

Rosacher did not care for the fact that Breque knew his business and he presumed the reason Breque had enlightened him was to make him aware that he was no longer in control. "Why have you come here?" he asked.

"I wish my visit could have been made under happier circumstances," said Breque. "Though I realize your relationship with Ludie must have been strained, to say the least, I imagine there likely is some residual emotional attachment."

"Get to the point, won't you?"

"She's dead," Breque said. "She went riding on East Crescent Road yesterday evening. Apparently she took a fall and split her head open on the rocks."

It was as if Rosacher's head had been enfolded in a warm cloth that muffled his senses. Moods swirled about him. At one moment he felt sorrowful, distressed to the point of tears, and the next relieved that she would no longer be a problem.

"Ludie?" he said. "Ludie's dead?"

"I'm afraid so."

"Who was with her?"

"To the best of my knowledge, she was alone. In recent years her drug use had increased to reckless proportions. Opiates, mainly. On several occasions, I'm told, she fell asleep while riding and took a tumble. I suppose that's what happened in this instance."

Anger flooded him, replacing the cold that had begun to hollow out his bones. "I don't give a damn what you suppose! Who stands to profit by her death? Has her will been read?"

"No, but I was a signatory to her last will a year or so ago," said Breque. "She may have had it reworked since, but I'm not aware of it. There were a number of small bequests, and she expressed the desire that her holdings in the company be placed in a public trust that would benefit the citizens of Morningshade."

That shocked Rosacher, being a breech of the agreement he had made with the Church in twenty-five years. "Who is to administer the trust?"

"A law firm. Lawrence, Behrens, Ecclestone and Associates. Are you familiar with them?"

Rosacher started to respond angrily, to say that this was the same firm who had handled his agreement with the Church, and to say further that the Church must have grown impatient; but caution threw up a flag. Had Ludie revealed the existence of the agreement to Breque? It was not inconceivable. If so, how did this play into Breque's visit? The Church was a patient monster—they had less than ten years left to wait and it would have taken an extreme provocation for them to break the agreement. While it was possible that Ludie had wanted to thumb her nose at the agreement between Rosacher and the Church by making such a will, it was highly unlikely that the firm that had drafted the agreement would have written such a will. All this led him to suspect that Breque was dissembling in some fashion. He felt suddenly heavy of limb and heart, a physical reaction not only to the news of Ludie's death, but to the realization that he was being pulled back into the drug business.

"The truth," he said. "Why have you come here today? What do you want?"

"Ludie died without revealing the process by which the blood is refined." Breque stretched out a leg and wiggled his foot, as if working out a kink. "We have enough mab on hand to satisfy our customers for two weeks or thereabouts. I need your assistance in making more."

That Ludie had kept the process—or rather the lack thereof—secret surprised Rosacher and muddied the waters further; but it had no bearing on what he needed to do to ensure his survival. He pretended to mull over the question and finally said, "I'll make more of the drug for you, but I have conditions."

Breque nodded. "I assumed as much. Proceed."

"Firstly, I want to see Ludie's will. Secondly, I am to be left alone in the treatment room. Under no circumstances will you or any of your agents seek to spy on me. If you violate this article of our pact, I will walk away and leave you to deal with thousands of unhappy addicts."

Breque started to speak, but Rosacher waved him to silence and continued: "Any attempt to extract information regarding the process by chicanery or force will set in motion certain mechanisms that will destroy the business. These mechanisms have been in place since the beginning of our relationship, and I have complete confidence in their efficacy. Do you understand?"

"Yes, of course," said Breque. "But I hope…"

"Thirdly, I believe your expansionist policies imperil the business. Therefore I wish to be consulted on all matters of foreign policy, particularly those relating to your attempts at expansion, whether in Temalagua or elsewhere. Should you fail to convince me of the rightness of your course and, despite this, continue along it, I will cease assisting you in the production of mab."

Incredulous, Breque said, "You're asking for a veto over any decision I make?"

"As they relate to foreign policy, yes. I'm assuming that you intend to expand in more than one direction and that you will need money to prosecute these conflicts. A great deal of money. I would be a fool not to want a voice in these decisions. I have a right to safeguard my investment."

"You leave me little choice," said Breque after a moment.

"Oh, you have options, but only one of them is worth your attention: the option of persuading me that you are choosing a direction that promises success. I have nothing against pursuing an expansionist foreign policy; however, I demand that it be done judiciously."

"You've made me wealthy...and powerful as well." Breque smiled, as though attempting to lighten the impact of what he said next. "I've little to entertain myself apart from dabbling in regional politics. A prudent soul might suggest that by thwarting me you're playing a dangerous game."

"If you're a fool, then you are correct—I am. But I don't believe you're a fool." Rosacher paused to allow a reponse. Breque blew out air through his lips, making a perturbed noise.

"One last thing," Rosacher said. "I imagine you must have operatives in places such as Alta Tiron and Mospiel, men and women capable of clandestine investigations."

"Of course."

"I'll need two of them for a period of...let's say three months. That should do the job. Preferably a man and a woman. I have no desire to conscript your best people, but I would welcome competence."

"How do you intend to use them?"

"You're an intelligent man, Jean-Daniel. Surely you can hazard a guess?"

"I'd say you're planning to look into Ludie's death. But why not use your own operatives?"

"I have no operatives, merely eyes and ears on the street. Your people are bound to be more efficient than anyone in my employ."

Following an exchange of patently fraudulent pleasantries, Breque left Rosacher to contemplate the view, but his contemplative mood was broken. He felt agitated, ill at ease. No matter how hard he tried he was unable to enfold himself in the landscape, to sink into it and become part of a harmonious whole. None of the particulars of his life seemed properly aligned. As he sat and stewed over a variety of trivial issues, he recognized that although it appeared that Breque had been neutralized, the councilman would continue to be a significant problem because he had fallen in love with power and Rosacher knew from experience that nothing, not even the threat of destruction, would discourage him from seeking more.

12

NTIL HIS MEETING WITH Breque, Rosacher's days had been relatively undemanding. He would spend a few hours handling logistical issues at the House and, once he was assured that things were running smoothly, he would pass the remainder of his time in reflection upon his newfound faith, an imperfect thing that he examined in various lights, trying alternately to shore it up and pick it apart. On occasion he was summoned back to the House to deal with some crisis, but these instances grew more infrequent as the men and women he had trained to be his aides grew more competent. Following the meeting, however, he was forced to spend hours each day in the treatment room, located beneath the amphitheater, there pretending to work some magic with the blood to make it suitable for human consumption. Since no one was permitted to oversee this process, he initially whiled away the hours by daydreaming and playing mental games; but he wearied of these pastimes and took to writing down his thoughts. Sitting in a wooden chair beside a ceramic-lined tub of Griaule's blood (which, against logic, gave no sign of congealing), staring at the the black cryptograms that materialized upon its golden surface, then faded and vanished, it was hardly surprising that his thoughts were of Griaule— insights into the dragon's intent, meditations on man's place in relation to Griaule and other like topics. Soon he began to organize these thoughts into essay form and, after several months of pruning and polishing, he read one of the essays, an examination of Griaule's influence upon the history of Teocinte entitled "On Our Dragon Nature," delivering it by means of a speaking tube that carried his raspy whisper throughout the amphitheater. The reaction was overhelming, outstripping his expectations—the gift shop was besieged with requests for printed copies of the essay and also with inquiries as to when the next "sermon" would be read. It seemed that a tremendous audience had been waiting for just such a preachment to give shape and substance to their inarticulate feelings, and so Rosacher was encouraged to construct a second essay. As he searched about for an appropriate topic, he cast his mind back to the beginning of his involvement with the dragon, to his study of the blood and the peculiar lapses in time (as if, he imagined, he had been skipped across the river of time like a flat stone across an actual river) that had marked the dragon's efforts to thwart that study. Viewed in retrospect, it was an unwieldy tactic. It would have been much easier for the dragon to arrange his death—he'd had ample weapons at his disposal. Yet instead of letting flakes or enemies or some other element of the natural world do his bidding, Griaule had imperiled Rosacher time and again only to save him for some mysterious purpose, perhaps the very purpose he was now serving, the deification of the dragon. It was as if through his interaction with humanity, Griaule had adopted a human means of problem-solving, a haphazard empiricism, trying this ploy, discarding another, rummaging through innumerable potentials until he had winnowed them down to a single promising thread, one that embodied an immortal perspective on mortal circumstance...and thus was Rosacher led to write the essay entitled, "Is The God I Worship The God I Cause To Be?", which elicited a more enthusiastic response than had his first attempt at theological discourse.

While visiting with Meric Cattanay on his tower one sunny, blustery afternoon, he brought up the subject, asking the artist if he had ever thought much about it. Cattanay was belted into a sturdy chair atop the platform, dabbing paints onto blank pages in a sketchpad, mixing colors together and adding linseed oil, then gauging the effect. He had aged markedly during the previous decade—his hair had gone from mostly gray to mostly white, the lines on his face had deepened into seams and his movements were stiff and halting, so much so that whenever the tower creaked in the wind, Rosacher would imagine the creaking issued from Cattanay's joints. He required assistance in order to ascend and descend from the tower—thus the chair. "I used to think a great deal about things of that sort," he said, wiping off a brush with a rag. "I never got anywhere with it. Too busy, I guess. And now I don't have the time. If the mural's going to be finished before I die, I'd better work swiftly."

"You're being overly dramatic," said Rosacher. "You've long years ahead of you."

Cattanay dunked the brush into a jar of cleansing solution. "I wish I could believe you, but I listen to what my body tells me…and it's telling me I don't have much longer. Both my parents were dead by their early sixties. Unlike yours, I'd wager. The years have been extremely kind to you." He selected a finer brush. "When I used to wonder about Griaule, whether he was a god, all that, I concluded that of course he was. What else could he be? He's the most godlike being I've ever run across and if there's a consensus about the question, which there seems to be, who am I to argue? I'm a simple craftsman and not a deep thinker—I'll leave that to you and Breque."

"You must have gone round and round about Griaule," said Rosacher. "I mean, you didn't just make a snap decision."

"I gave it due consideration." Cattanay dipped the brush in indigo, daubed it onto the page, and mumbled something that Rosacher didn't catch. "The truth is," he went on, "once I stopped thinking about Griaule as a metaphysical problem, I became more content. I realized that a lot of what had been bothering me...you know, woman troubles, logistical matters, and so forth. I had complicated them by paying so much attention to Griaule. It was more satisfying to focus on questions I had the ability to answer. For instance." He showed Rosacher the page on which he'd been painting— a splotch of gold partly limned in indigo. "I've been debating whether or not to edge the lower right quadrant of the mural with indigo. It wouldn't serve as a border. It wouldn't be this neat. Just a ragged evolution of the paint from gold to indigo in this one area. What do you think?"

Rosacher studied the page. "Maybe. I don't know."

"Of course you don't. To make a judgment, you'd need to have some expertise, you'd need to understand how the color would work on the scales. You'd have to learn about varnishes. I've been using beeswax to fix the colors, but I've been considering a more conventional finish on the indigo." He chuckled. "You're not qualified to make that sort of decision. And none of us are

165

qualified to assess Griaule's mystical potential. Let it go. Concentrate on the things you're expert in. You'll be much happier."

"I've become expert on how to handle whores." Rosacher said glumly. "And drugs. I know how to create a demand for drugs."

"You're a businessman," said Cattanay. "And a scientist. Perhaps you should focus on science for a while. Stop worrying about Griaule."

Rosacher suppressed a laugh. "I'm afraid that science is entwined with metaphysics in this case."

The old man's white hair lashed about in the wind and he groped for his beret, lying on the platform beside the chair. Rosacher handed it to him.

"When you go down," Cattanay said. "And I'm not trying to run you off. But when you do go, you may see a redheaded boy standing by the tower. Ask him to bring up a blanket, won't you?" He turned to a fresh page in his sketchbook and looked toward the lowering sun, halfway obscured by Griaule's majestic head. "Astonishing...to be sitting here. I hoped I might open my own gallery, sell a few of my paintings. I certainly wouldn't have predicted that I'd be fortunate enough to have witnessed all that I have. You ever think you'd see anything like him?"

"Yes, I did," said Rosacher. "But I thought it would be different."

✛

THOUGH MUCH OF what Cattanay said rang true, Rosacher failed to follow his advice. Encouraged by the reception given his essays, he embarked upon the creation of one a week (a task that entailed his working many late nights), and read it aloud to those assembled in the amphitheater each Friday evening prior to the weekend bacchanal. The most pronounced effect of these essays was not, as might be surmised, upon the audience, but was their effect upon Rosacher himself. Before taking up the pen, he had reached the conclusion that the dragon exerted a powerful influence on human affairs, but his belief was based upon a preponderance of evidence, rarely rising to the level of faith, and he was constantly assailed by doubt; but with every word written and spoken, his belief in Griaule's divinity was strengthened and transformed into a devout reverence, until he became as zealous in his affirmation of the dragon's divine potency as he had once been in his determination to paint Griaule as an exemplar of the mundane, somewhat larger than most, yet ordinary nonetheless.

Rosacher's investigation into Ludie's death proved fruitless. Her will, as he had presumed, was a sham, and either the killer had covered his tracks too well or else the accident had been no more than an accident; but he was confident that Breque knew of his agreement to hand over the business to the Church and that he was attempting to turn him against Mospiel in hopes that he would abrogate the agreement. Each week brought a fresh complaint from Breque's office—the prelates wanted a larger percentage of the foreign markets or demanded a tightening of quality control or else were creating a fuss about some trivial issue that they claimed ran contrary to their doctrine. Rosacher advised Breque to appease them by offering a crumb of what they asked for, and Breque did as advised; yet he kept up his saber-rattling and made bellicose gestures against adjoining countries, massing troops along their borders and holding training exercises. Rosacher felt that something would have to be done to muzzle Breque's ambitions, but he decided to bide his time. Though the relationship was sorely taxed on occasion, Breque had proved himself a dependable and trustworthy partner, one to whom Rosacher owed much of his success. Not the least of this debt related to Amelita Sobral, one of the operatives that Rosacher had borrowed from Breque in order to investigate Ludie's death. She was a slender, black-haired woman with a milky complexion and features of an unearthly delicacy (enormous dark eyes, tiny chin, high cheekbones, a face that might have been the work of a master carver with a bent for the exotic) that lent her a deceptively frail, fey manner, like a fairy tale maiden in constant need of rescue, though this was far from the case, and a manner so grave, it challenged Rosacher to extract a smile from her. He assumed that she and her male counterpart would inform Breque about his activities, and his deeper motive in requesting them was to control the stream of information between his office and Breque's by feeding them material and having his own agents report on what the operatives had communicated to Breque. In particular he wished to learn by this experiment whether Breque would react to false information about the murder investigation and thus prove himself complicit in Ludie's death.

Amelita and Rosacher became lovers shortly after she entered his employ. He had thought this would happen, and that it would be entirely cynical on her part, but he allowed the relationship to prosper because it suited his strategy and further because he was smitten with her. Yet he noticed over the months that the information she passed on to Breque excluded details designed to inflame the councilman and eventually became an uninformative digest of what Rosacher permitted her to see. One drizzly morning almost two years after he had requested her services, she came to him out on the ledge, where he had gone to write and to draw inspiration from the shifting pastorale visible from Griaule's side. She wore the khaki trousers of a Hangtown woman and a blouse of black broadcloth, a garment that signaled self-abnegation among her people, puritanical cultists who dwelled along the banks of the Putomaya in the jungly lowlands of the country. Sitting with her knees drawn up beneath her chin, she confessed her betrayal, telling him that she had reported to Breque on Rosacher's activities—as her feelings for Rosacher grew, however, she had come to censor her reports, omitting whatever she considered to be crucial, but she could no longer maintain even this level of subterfuge. He was unable to rid himself of suspicion and, though moved by her apparent sincerity, with a fraction of his mind he reserved judgment, knowing her to be an accomplished deceiver—he thought the confession might be a ploy designed to engage his trust. He drew her into an embrace and, his face buried in her hair, said that he loved her, words he fervently believed as he spoke them, but that seemed devalued once he released her.

"I should never have accepted the assignment," she said in a small voice. "My instincts told me to avoid you at all costs."

"Then we would have never met," Rosacher said. "Would you have preferred that?"

"It might have been for the best."

"We can move past this," he said.

"I'm not so sure."

"Well, I am!"

"I have higher standards for my behavior than do you...or so it would seem."

He tried to read her face, but it remained impassive. "What would you have me do?" he asked. "Devise some punishment? You were following orders and deserve none. Forgive you? I forgive you. That should go without saying."

She gave him a penetrating look, then hung her head, picking at a fray on her trouser cuff. At last she said, "You're taking this rather well...and I find it odd that you don't seem at all surprised by my duplicity."

"Did you expect me to put on a show for you? Wail and tear my hair? I'm not a fool. I knew from the outset that you might be carrying tales about me back to Breque."

"I see. You were being duplicitous as well."

"Naturally I protected myself. I don't know whether I would call that duplicity. If I had mentioned my suspicions concerning you, it would have ended our relationship. I wasn't prepared for it to end."

Rain plip-plopped on the scales, dripping from the edge of the wing, and an assortment of trivial creatures were poking their heads, feelers and other protuberances up between Griaule's scales. Amelita absorbed what he had said and then made a slight gesture with her head that might have been a nod signaling acceptance.

"I have one question regarding Breque," he said. "Did you ever withhold information from me that would have implicated him in Ludie's murder?"

"I found nothing to implicate him," she said. "That scarcely constitutes proof of innocence, but if he was involved, he left no trace."

Rosacher could not hide his disappointment and she put a hand on his arm, saying, "I'll keep tryng to find a connection, if you wish."

"No, just keep doing what you're doing."

"What do you mean?"

"Keep turning in your reports to Breque."

A bewildered expression crossed her face. "You want me to continue deceiving him?"

"Your deceit protects us. If you were to go to Breque and tell him you could no longer work for him, he would simply replace you with someone whom I might not be able to detect."

Seeing that she was displeased, he said, "You became entangled in this web when you embarked upon a course of deception. It's going to take some time for you to free yourself."

"And so, in order to 'free myself,' I must cease being Breque's creature and become yours? Or have I always been your creature? You knew I was a spy from the outset, didn't you? You used me!"

"What would you have done in my place? Breque put me in the position of having to defend myself. I blame him, not you."

A squabbling arose from the nests hanging beneath the edge of the wing, and one of them, large and mud-colored, its bottom shaped roughly like a four-pointed star, swayed back and forth. A spasm of frustration struck through Rosacher and he aimed a punch at the scale whereon he sat, but pulled it before impact, recalling the damage done his hand by similar punches thrown in the past.

"Damn it!" he said. "You're the most contrary human being I've ever come across!"

For all her reaction, he might have spoken under his breath. She stared into the middle distance, giving no sign of noticing the flight of swifts that swooped low across the dragon's back, passing with a rush of wings a few feet away. Rosacher waited to see how long it would take her to speak, but lost count of the seconds. Three minutes or thereabouts, he reckoned.

"So if we are to continue," she said, "whatever house we build will rest upon a foundation of lies."

"That's all you take from this conversation? That dire prognosis."

She remained silent and turned her head to the side, away from him, as if something to the south had caught her attention.

"Well," he said curtly. "At least we have a foundation."

FOR THE LIFE of him, Rosacher could not fathom why he loved Amelita. In truth, he was unsure that what he felt was love, but he was most certainly obsessed with her. Thanks to mab, every woman was beautiful, but Amelita's beauty, in his view, was supernal. Each line and curve of her had a sculptural velocity, a flow that led the eye from one place to the next, and whenever she moved it seemed to Rosacher that he had witnessed something wholly of nature, like the movement of wheat in the wind. She was a vigorous and attentive lover, and on those rare occasions when the clouds lifted and her mood brightened, she became vivacious and clever, given to quick-witted repartee; but she was depressed the majority of the time and often he would find her weeping for no reason she could articulate. There was, he thought, a great blank space in his relationship with her, a crucial vacancy that prevented them from perfecting their union. He surmised that the moral and physical rectitude of her childhood was to blame, but since she would speak of it only in the vaguest of generalities, he was unable to connect cause to effect in any practical way and thus incapable of concocting a remedy. As a result, his scrutiny of her grew more focused, more obsessive.

Not long after this conversation, they moved into an apartment atop the House of Griaule, one that until then had been reserved for visiting dignitaries, and there they lived for the next three years. The opulence of the place cheered Amelita. She would wander through the rooms, trailing her hand across the backs of gilt chairs and sofas upholstered with cloth that presented a dragon motif; she would sit and study the ornately worked tops of teak tables inlaid with mother-of-pearl by the light of brass lamps mounted on the walls, and gaze intently at the icy, delicate chandelier in the living room, as if she saw in its prismatic depths a kind of resolution. Rosacher could not be certain that these luxurious appointments actually increased her happiness, but they did appear

LUCIUS SHEPARD

to lift her out of herself, to satisfy some vital need, for her tears no longer flowed so easily and she developed an interest in the fauna that occupied Griaule—indeed, she began to go for day-long walks about the dragon, sketching the creatures that she spotted (marvelously complicated sketches that displayed a heretofore unexploited talent for art), and collecting them in a folio, along with her written observations. Her favorite room in the apartment was their bedchamber. It was dominated by a richly carved ebony four-poster mounted on a dais, with a painted canopy (more dragons) and peach-colored satin sheets; but the main attraction for Amelita was the carpet, an intricate weave of reds, purples, gray and white imported from Isfahan. The design was partitioned into two large hemispheres like, she said, an ancient map of an imaginary world, and once she had formulated this connection, she broke off her nature walks and would lie in bed all day sketching the fantastic creature with which her mind populated that world. Rosacher did not think this inactivity was good for her health, either mental or physical, and urged her to start walking again; but she would not budge and told him she found this type of art more creative and inspiring, and assured him that she was content. Before too long, however, her bouts of weeping grew more frequent and prolonged, and her moods darkened to the point that he feared she might take her own life. Her face began to betray signs of aging—faint crowsfeet, a worry line on the bridge of the nose—whereas his face, the undamaged portion of it, betrayed none, and he was led to consider the possibility that this discrepancy might be a factor in her despair.

One day while he sat beside a twenty-gallon tub of golden blood in the treatment room, entranced by its shifting patterns, it occurred to him that the reason for his lack of aging might be the massive injection of the dragon's blood given him by the late Arthur Honeyman. And if such were the case, if a huge dose of the blood ameliorated the signs of aging and, perhaps, increased one's longevity. If the effect were not peculiar to him, he could give a similar dose to Amelita and, once she became aware of its effect, that might have the secondary effect of enlivening her. None of this struck him with the force of a revelation—they were idle thoughts, merely—but he kept returning to them, re-examining them, and they acquired a revelatory power. Here was the answer to a question he had asked himself for decades: why had Griaule sought to distract him from his work? If he had arrived at this conclusion early on (it seemed impossible now that he had not) and, whether correct or incorrect, that conclusion had become known, there would have been a run on the blood by those desiring a longer prime of life. Despite his vast bulk, Griaule would have been drained, his veins and arteries emptied. Did the fact that the dragon had ceased distracting him from these ideas portend that he was prepared to die, or did he now trust in Rosacher's devotion and so had offered up the remedy of his blood as a blessing to reward him for his faith? A myriad doctrinal questions attendant on that initial question arose, all of them casting doubt on his basic assumption, but in his eagerness to find a cure for his relationship with Amelita and to bring her the gift of an extended youth, he brushed them aside. That night, as she lay on their bed, naked beneath the peach-colored sheets, he sat next to her and spoke about his experience with the blood and explained what he intended to do, showing her a full syringe. She took the syringe from him and peered at the fluid—in the unsteady lantern light, the dark characters of the blood surfaced and faded with the elusiveness of eels, staying only long enough to give an impression of sinuous vigor before slipping away into their golden medium.

"Is this something you want?" she asked. "Am I not sufficiently beautiful?"

He had expected this kind of joyless reaction and advised her that the blood would not enhance her looks, merely maintain them longer than was usual.

"But is this what *you* want?"

"I thought it would please you," he said. "Doesn't every women wish to prolong her beauty?"

"I've always been beautiful," she said. "I think it would be interesting to grow old and wrinkled."

Impatient with her, he tried to take back the syringe; but she resisted him playfully and tucked the syringe beneath a pillow.

"Prove you love me," she said. "And I'll give it back."

"After all these years," he said, "I shouldn't have to prove anything."

"'All these years?'" Her playful mien evaporated. "Has it been such a chore? Putting up with me?"

"You know that's not what I meant."

She looked at him soberly. "You amaze me, Richard. You continually amaze me."

He sought to make a joke of her comment. "That's been my aim."

"Well, you've succeeded. You're a brothel keeper, a drug dealer, and you're ruthless in your business practices. You've had people murdered. Yet you think of yourself as a good man. Most people are no different. We all engage in that sort of deceit, but we're not as skilled at it as you. Your sins are so great, yet you hide the fact from yourself so thoroughly! It's truly remarkable."

Her words sliced into him and he said, "Damn it, 'lita! Must our pleasure always be held hostage to your morbid outlook on life."

He made another try for the syringe and she pushed him away, this time with considerable force.

"You're not a good man," she said. "You don't love me...except in the way most people love, and that isn't really love, but a form of self-aggrandisement. I wish I had your talent for hiding from myself, for ignoring the realities—then I could love you the way you pretend to love me."

"Then why are you with me? The money...is that it? The power. Do you find it exhilarating?"

"What I find exhilarating is that you're so adept at deluding yourself, sometimes I'm able to believe the fairy tales you tell yourself."

He wanted to reject her argument, her characterization of his feelings, but knew that to do so would only anger her further. Even if he submitted to her logic, she would be likely to mine a cause for disagreement from whatever he said.

She pulled back the sheet to expose a creamy thigh and pointed to it with the syringe. "This is where you would inject me?"

"Yes," he said, encouraged—he thought she was relenting, deciding to relent, to allow them to go forward. "I'll do it in the big muscle. It'll sting, and there'll be a sensation of cold, but that doesn't last."

"Apart from you," she said, "has anyone else been injected with so much of the blood?"

"No, but I've adjusted the dose to compensate for your lighter weight. It should be perfectly safe."

As he said those words, he realized how irresponsible it was not to do some further testing, and he reached again for the syringe; but she blocked him with her knee and jammed the needle home, thumbing down the plunger.

"Let's see," she said, and appeared on the verge of saying more, but the blood overpowered her and all that emerged from her throat was the shadow of a sound, the faintest of gasps.

He had thought she would react as had he and that as she recovered she would grow fuddled and amorous; instead she sat up in bed, more alert than he had seen her in months and, dismissing his expressions of concern with a blithe gesture, she strolled about the room, inspecting gilt picture frames, touching the surface of a mirror as though to validate that it was her reflection she saw, caressing the sublime curves of a divan that had been owned by a Byzantine prince, and eventually coming to stand at the center of the carpet, directly between the two hemispheres, posed with her head turned to the side, her high, small breasts and full hips lacquered with gleams, her left hand touching her left shoulder, strangely demure despite her nudity. Whether due to a physical transformation caused by the blood or a perceptual distortion on Rosacher's part, her body appeared enveloped in a white radiance, and this aura, this glow, spread from her feet across the complex patterns of her imaginary world, a puddle of light making it look as if the bloom of her beauty was the production of a luminous essence that had been imprisoned until now within the threads of the carpet.

Rosacher waited for her to speak, scarcely breathing, half-convinced that when she gave tongue to her thoughts, it would be oracular in nature...but rather than speaking she sprang for the door, grabbed up a gray cloak from a chair and enfolded herself in it, and fled the apartment. Stunned, caught off guard, he hesitated before chasing after her and she disappeared down the stairs—he did not catch sight of her again until twenty-five minutes later when, after searching through the House, questioning the passers-by he encountered in the corridors, he reached the front entrance where she was pointed out to him by a group of young men loitering on the steps. Visible in the strong moonlight, she had ascended to a platform atop the scaffolding braced against Griaule's side—it still bore tatters of black bunting from Meric Cattanay's funeral six weeks earlier—and was scrambling toward the joint of the dragon's shoulder, using vines to haul herself upward, moving with such agility and grace that he was hard put to believe this was the same woman who had been more-or-less bedridden for months. Ignoring the young men's catcalls, he ran to the base of the scaffolding and clambered up it, but realized that he could not match her pace and slowed his ascent, using a measure of caution in securing his footing. By the time he had climbed to the platform, she had disappeared into the thickets atop Griaule's back, yet he kept going, fueled by a sense of desperation, plowing through brush and tangles of vines. As he skirted the limits of Hangtown, the lights of Martita's fractioned by leaves and branches, he wondered what she could have in mind. Was she driven by delirium? She hadn't seemed delirious, but rather focused and serene...but she may have gone mad after fleeing their bedchamber. And what was that glow emanating from her body? She hadn't looked to be glowing any longer, so perhaps it had been a flaw in his vision, some mental defect brought on by stress. Be that as it may, her reaction to the blood had been completely different from his, that much was certain, and he feared for her.

He checked the ledge beneath the wing and called out to the shadows deeper in. Nothing, no response. He proceeded farther along the dragon's spine. If she were headed for the plain below, he might never find her. He shouted her name and listened to the winded silence that came back to him. The brush grew thicker and his step faltered when he moved past the point where the spine began to slope downward. Only the boldest of scalehunters ventured beyond this area—he remembered old Jarvis telling him that something big lived in the thickets above the haunch, some kind of animal, possibly a bear, that could tear you apart—remains of its victims had been found and there had been a handful of sightings, albeit fleeting and unreliable ones. Of course that had been years before and it might be that the animal had gone elsewhere or had died, but Rosacher had learned it was unwise to disregard such warnings, because more often than not the consequences of flouting them proved severe. The moon, silvery and almost full, was at its zenith and in its light he could make out palm crowns on the plain below, but not their trunks.

A thin mist veiled the brilliance of the stars. Insects chirred and a nightjar cried. Rosacher felt as alone and frightened as he had on that long-ago night when he had drawn blood from Griaule's tongue, yet he pressed forward into the thickets, made wary by every rustle, every shadowy twitch and tremble of leaf or twig.

Another quarter of an hour brought him to what was essentially a bald patch on the dragon's back, an oval area some fifty or sixty feet across, and perhaps much larger than that (he couldn't judge how far it stretched down the slope of Griaule's side), scantily covered in dirt and weeds, but free of brush. He stepped out onto it and understood the reason for the lack of vegetation. Some idiot had cleared it away—within the past year, he guessed—and attempted to pry loose the enormous scales, shattering them into dozens of pieces that shifted under his weight. The danger associated with trespassing in places like this was that Griaule might mistake you for a scalehunter come to violate his body, and though Rosacher believed the dragon capable of distinguishing among humans and had evidence aplenty that Griaule recognized him for who he was, that belief was nothing he cared to rely on in this situation. Best, he decided, to go to Martita's, have a glass of ale and think things over. Perhaps he could prevail upon the scalehunters there to assist him in the search. And then he spied Amelita. She stood facing away from him, her figure obscured by the gray cloak, so low on the dragon's side, some twenty yards distant, that if she took another step or two forward, she would be unable to keep her footing.

"'lita!" he shouted.

The cloak flapped about her, appearing to register a stronger force of wind than the one blowing across the dragon's back. An updraft, he thought. He shouted again and she turned toward him. At that distance he could not distinguish her features, but her skin had acquired the mousey coloration of the cloak. Tentaively, realizing something was wrong, he walked forward a half-dozen paces, paused, and then went a few paces more. Not only had her complexion gone gray, but a myriad fine lines now webbed her skin, as if she had grown ancient as she fled from him—yet on second glance she did not seem to have aged, but rather that her youthful image had been partitioned into irregular segments like those of a jigsaw puzzle. He spoke her name again, less a shout than a plaintive inquiry. The wind blew more fiercely about her—at least her hair (also gray) billowed and the cloak flapped with increased fury—but Rosacher felt no like increase where he stood and heard no keening or any other windy noise. Cold gripped the nape of his neck, as if it had been seized by a dead hand. He backed away, his heel catching on a loosened fragment, and he pitched onto his side, his temple smacking down hard. He must have blacked out, for when his eyes blinked open he discovered her standing over him. He thought initially that her facial muscles were in spasm, but her expression was neither agonized or contorted—it was her customary stoic expression, reflecting no particular mood or attitude. And then he realized it wasn't her muscles that were moving—it was the skin, and not just that of her face. Every square inch of skin was rippling the way bacon ripples in a frying pan. Each tiny segment of skin as defined by the cracks pulsed to a separate rhythm, as if they were blistering, about to release a vile fluid. A dribble of sound leaked from him, a whimper born of fear, fear for himself, for her, revulsion. He crawled away, trying to regain his feet...but fell again. Her lips parted, her eyelids drooped and she lifted an arm, a gesture that an opera singer might make in straining for a high note, and something fluttered up light as ash from the back of her hand, something winged—it fluttered in the air above her. Further gray scraps disengaged from her and joined it, accumulating into a cluster, then a cloud that bobbled and danced overhead. Each time a scrap lifted from her body, it left behind a patch of glistening flesh that rapidly darkened and began to pulse. She was dissolving, disintegrating...the process quickened, quickened again, and after two or three minutes more she became unrecognizable, diminished to a stump, a gray stalagmite from which winged things no larger than a flake emerged and arose, forming a whirling mass that encircled Rosacher, penning him in. Possessed by dread, he knew that once she had completely dissolved, these remnants would descend, fasten onto his face and kill him with their stings. But in the end only one of the creatures touched him. It hovered in front of his face for an instant and, his mind bright with terror, he had the impression that its wings were not attached to an insect body, but to a slender white female figure, perfect in every detail, a replica in miniature of his former lover—it brushed against his cheek, imparting a chill sensation, and flew up to merge with the fluttering gray cloud, which then passed toward the south, vanishing behind the bulge of Griaule's spine.

For several minutes thereafter, Rosacher continued lying where he had fallen. The chill spread across his cheek, yet did not disturb him—on the contrary, the coolness was soothing, as though a salve had been applied. The bizarre manner of Amelita's death, if death it had been, if she were not reincarnate as a cluster of flakes, left him in an uncertain mood, overcome by sorrow, but also wondering if this might not have been the best possible outcome for her—she had always been unhappy—and not merely unhappy, despondent, despairing—except for moments here and there, and though he ached for her, he experienced an undercurrent of relief that she had been released from whatever pain had been gnawing at her for all her days—but this did not alleviate his own pain. He wept while walking back to Martita's and had to pause outside the door in order to compose himself. Once inside, seated at a table in the rear, he hated the dim, wavering lantern light, the smell of stale beer, the lively talk and laughter around him, all the dull brown normalcy of the place. He hung his head and tried to calm himself, but his thoughts flurried and he kept picturing Amelita as her living layers peeled away, her mouth open and eyes lidded, an expression that reminded him of how she had looked when they made love—yet it lacked vitality and was absent the sounds of passion, the gasps, the musical sighs, and thus seemed a mockery.

Martita dropped onto the bench opposite, bubbly as ever, and asked what brought him to her door—it had been months since he visited. "You'll be wanting a mug of the brown, I suppose," she said, and before he could answer, she put a hand to her mouth. "God! What happened to your face?"

"My face?" he said. "What's wrong with it? Am I bleeding?"

She told him to wait, ran to the bar and brought back a small mirror that she kept beneath the counter. "You won't believe this unless you see for yourself," she said, holding it out to him.

In its clouded surface he saw his old face, his face as it had been before Ludie and Honeyman betrayed him, unmarked by any scarring, marred only by the lines of middle age. And he understood...or perhaps he didn't understand, perhaps he only hoped he understood why the sting of that tiny creature pared from her life had felt so soothing. Moved by that flawed comprehension, then, he once again began to weep.

13

AMELITA'S DEATH INSPIRED A period of self-reflection in Rosacher that neither illuminated nor provided surcease. Though his love for her may have been tainted, poisoned by his manipulative spirit, his grief seemed real enough. It was a black cancer gnawing at his heart, decaying his thoughts. He did not believe there would be an end to it, and he foresaw a future in which would be forced to dwell beneath a self-woven shroud, mired in a gloom that blotted out life's exuberant particularity. He shut himself away in the apartment, lying in the bed he had shared with Amelita, the curtains drawn, wanting to deny even the possibility of light, praying that this darkness would somehow keep him connected to her darkness. He had no wish to work, no desire for food or drink, and when he smoked mab, it merely enriched and deepened his personal shadows. He punished himself for becoming angry with her the night she died, for a myriad lesser transgressions, and for being so preoccupied with her, for doting on her now more with greater intensity than he had when she was alive. He then came to hate himself for doubting the authenticity of his grief. He also hated himself for conflating his obsession with the dragon with everything from philosophical questions to practical considerations (would Griaule approve of this or that, etc.) and for having constructed a seemingly flimsy metaphysics about the beast that no amount of speculation or denial could dissolve. He supposed that if he were to look out and see that gargantuan foreleg rising above, he would hate the dragon as well, but he didn't have the energy to crack the window and prove his thesis.

He passed long hours poring over Amelita's sketchbooks, searching for clues to her character, and discovered a rendering of a gray winged creature with a woman's body, with pale skin and small, high breasts and cascading black hair. She had drawn this same creature half-a-dozen times—the last drawing was very nearly a self-portrait and was inscribed with the words, "the aurelia phase." A few lines of text followed, stating that the creature derived its nourishment from the crepuscular light of pre-dawn and dusk. Amelita's usage of "aurelia" was unfamiliar to him—he learned that the word was not just a name, but was also used to denote a chrysalis.

He had almost convinced himself that the creature was a hallucination, a byproduct of his fright, but the drawing overthrew that assumption and he was forced to struggle with the notion that Amelita had been transformed into a swarm of flakes and that she might pass from this stage into yet another, perhaps more repellent stage. This in turn caused him to wonder whether she had anticipated the transformation, or if Griaule had plucked the idea from her brain and made it into a reality. That thought, and a hundred attendant thoughts redolent of his obsession with the dragon, renewed his self-loathing and sank him to fresh depths of darkness and despair.

Breque visited him from time to time, staying but briefly, and eight months after Amelita's death he brought with him a thick folder that he deposited on the floor beside him. He sat in a gilt chair next to the bed and appeared to study Rosacher, who lay beneath the peach-colored sheets, clad in a robe that had gone unwashed for weeks. Stubble dirtied Rosacher's cheeks, his hair was matted, and the bed was littered with open wine bottles (some were only partly empty and as a result the sheets were mapped with purplish stains). Breque cleared his throat and, when Rosacher did not react, he said, "I see that nothing has changed with you. Would you like me to leave?"

"Yes...unless you have pressing business," Rosacher said. "I've been keeping up with the production of mab and the House more-or-less runs itself. If your visit has nothing to do with our enterprise, I'm not in the mood to chat."

"From where I'm sitting, it looks as though you're in the mood to fart and scratch your bedsores…but not much else."

Rosacher said nothing.

"Very well," Breque said. "I have a proposal for you. It may be pressing, but I'm not sure I'd call it 'business'." Breque wrinkled his nose. "It stinks in here."

"Another reason for you to leave." Rosacher rolled onto his side to face the wall. "Anyway, I like it—it's my stink."

"When's the last time you allowed someone in to clean?"

"Goodbye," said Rosacher.

After a prolonged silence Breque said, "We've known each other for many years, Richard. We aren't always on the same side of an issue, but we've learned to practice the art of compromise with one another and I…"

"Do you actually think this is instructive?" Rosacher made a disparaging noise. "At any rate, you're the one who's compromised, not I."

"Have it your way. Whatever the case, we've helped each other over some rough patches and I dare say we've forged a strong friendship."

"Friendship?" Rosacher turned to Breque. "Don't make me laugh!"

"Are you asserting that you're not my friend?"

"Did I hurt your feelings? I'm sorry, I assumed you were joking. Every human interaction I know of is based upon greed...or the desire for security. Which is merely a more pernicious form of greed. By that criteria, you could say that cobras and hedgehogs are friends."

"If we're not friends, how would you characterize our relationship?"

"A criminal association leavened by certain social obligations. You'd have to be a fool to think it's anything more."

"Then I must be a fool." Breque crossed his legs and shifted about in the chair until he was comfortable. "I value you as an ally and a friend. And that's why I'm here. To suggest that you utilize my friendship and heed my advice."

"Oh, I can't wait to hear your advice." Rosacher sat up and made a show of adjusting pillows behind his back. "There! I'm ready to receive the benefit of your vast experience and wisdom."

"You need to busy yourself. Find something that challenges you and set yourself to overcome it."

Rosacher rolled his eyes. "Next you'll be telling me to adopt a puppy and learn to love again."

"Your period of mourning, if that's what this is, has damaged..."

"What else would it be?"

"I don't doubt that you mourn for Amelita. I understand that you loved her. But mourning is a process that should not entail you becoming subsumed by a memory. You've never been what I'd call a happy person..."

Rosacher gave a sardonic laugh. "Now there's a revelation!"

"...but neither have you been especially gloomy. Yet you've adopted Amelita's defeatism, her absolute pessimism, and made these qualities into a kind of memorial."

"It could be I've realized she was right about things."

"Or perhaps you're enjoying your misery. Indulging it. Her death provides you with a wonderful excuse for failure."

"Get out!"

"No," said Breque. "I don't think I will. I think I'll stay right here and watch you drink yourself into a stupor, or however else you plan to spend the day. Perhaps I'll take notes on your decay. I may want to write a biography on the topic some day, a paper containing my speculations as to whether the rotting away of the soul preceeds the rotting of the flesh, or vice versa."

The silence and dimness of the room seemed to combine into a heavy mantle that draped itself about Rosacher's shoulders. "What do you want of me?" he asked.

"I've brought you a project," said Breque. "It's a problem in a field of knowledge about which you know very little, but I'm confident that you can resolve it in our favor. The quality I admire most in you, Richard, is your ability to cut through the fat and get to the meat of an issue." He picked up the folder and placed it on the bed. "There's a lot of fat here, but I'm hopeful that you'll be able to cut through it swiftly."

"A project, eh?" Rosacher poked the folder with a forefinger, as if he expected it to bite. "Tell me about it."

"The folder contains plans, maps, and a number of suggestions offered by the former head of the militia regarding..."

"Corley? I wouldn't trust the worth of any suggestions he had to offer."

"I'm referring to General Aldo."

"Aldo? He's a competent leader, somewhat impetuous, but an excellent strategist. What happened? Did you demote him? If so, that was not wise."

"He proved too impetuous for his own good. He took a troop across the Temalaguan border two weeks ago—against my orders—and was killed in a skirmish."

"Who has taken over command? Mees would be my choice."

"Mees contracted a severe case of fever when he was last in the south. He'll be bedridden for several weeks. Thusfar I've been unable to find a suitable replacement."

Rosacher hissed in frustration. "Aldo may have disobeyed orders, but you always pressured him to be more aggressive. This has to be laid at your feet."

"I readily admit that some of the problem is due to a miscalculation on my part, but now is not the time to assign blame. We have to devise a means of forestalling the combined aggression of Temalagua and Mospiel."

"What are you saying? They're acting in concert?"

Breque nodded. "My operatives have reported that they have been planning an assault on Teocinte for the past several weeks. I notified Aldo and this…" He tapped the folder. "This is the plan he had begun working on when he died."

"What in God's name did you do to get us into this mess? Mospiel and Temalagua would never have joined forces unless you gave them extreme provocation. There must have been more to it than an ill-conceived foray into Temalagua."

"It's as I said, I miscalculated. We can discuss the extent of my malfeasance and what portion of blame attaches to me at a later date. It's imperative now that we construct a defense against the attack. We have a month to achieve this, possibly less, possibly a bit more."

"A month."

"Approximately. Aldo estimated that we might be able to count on six weeks at the outside…unless we're able to create a diversion that slows down their preparations."

"You've finally got what you wanted," Rosacher said bitterly. "A full-fledged war…and against two of our enemies, not one. My congratulations."

"Whatever their past differences, Mospiel join-ing forces with Temalagua was an inevitability. So Aldo believed. All the skirmish did was accelerate the timetable."

A feeling of malaise crept over Rosacher—it was as if he were being lowered into a tepid bath that dulled his senses and heavied his limbs. "Maybe we should put our fate in Griaule's hands. If he could save a nation from certain disaster, that would be the ultimate proof of his divinity. And if not, we deserve to be slaughtered for our reliance on a false god."

"That is precisely why I've brought Aldo's papers to you." Breque leaned forward in his chair, a new intensity in his voice. "Of all the people I have known, you have the strongest connection with Griaule. Over and over again his will has manifested in your life, and each time a miracle of sorts has transpired. I realize you've had occasion to doubt this, but I'm certain that beneath your doubt lies an indestructible core of faith. You've become Griaule's chosen weapon against all that threatens him."

Though Rosacher would have been amused by these words years before, he was flattered by them now; yet Breque had never been much for flattery and his stance toward the dragon was pragmatic—since almost everyone believed in Griaule's potency, he paid those beliefs lip service. Such was Rosacher's take on the man, anyway, and this was borne out by the sense that there had been a glint of falsity in Breque's fervent delivery.

"I never took you for a believer," Rosacher said.

Breque sat back in the chair. "You may consider me a recent covert."

Definitely a hint of falsity, perhaps even a degree of smugness, as if Breque felt that he had succeeded in his mission. Rosacher was tempted to deny him his success.

"My belief in Griaule has been predicated to a great degree by having observed you over the years," Breque said. "I have never been a zealot. Indeed, I am not one now. But I would be an idiot if I were to ignore the evidence before me, evidence that tells me you're the one man who can resolve this situation in our favor."

The conversation continued in this vein for several minutes more, with Breque expressing confidence in him and Rosacher demurring. Once the councilman had left, Rosacher decided he did not like being coerced, cajoled by flattery, and let the folder lie for the next three days; but Breque's words, the councilman's assertion that he, Rosacher, had been chosen for this work, had taken hold on him and at last he opened the folder, spreading its contents on his bed: maps, details on troop concentrations and where they were deployed, estimates of weaponry available to the armies of Temalagua and Mospiel, analyses of the strengths of their key military leaders. In sum, they painted a bleak picture of Teocinte's prospects for mounting a successful defense. From his reading of Aldo's marginal notes, Rosacher discovered that Aldo had favored a pre-emptive attack on Mospiel. Such a strike stood little chance of succeeding, but it would cause confusion amongst the enemy, and where confusion ruled, there a perspicacious general might find a critical opportunity.

Dismayed by what he had read, Rosacher relapsed into despondency and drank a bottle and a half of wine. His thoughts went once more to Amelita, and he was pulled back into a morass of guilt and desolation. But on the following morning, before he could sink beneath the surface of grief, he had a second look through the folder. There was no point in revisiting the assessments of their enemies' martial potential, so he focused on Aldo's marginalia and several pages from a journal kept during his foray into Temalagua on which Aldo had scribbled some notes. The notes made little sense to Rosacher, mainly consisting of groupings of two or three words, and sometimes only a single word, but his instincts told him to keep searching. One entry near the end of the journal came to intrigue him: a name, Bruno Cerruti, punctuated by three exclamation points. Written on the page close by the name were the words, "the hunt," and lower on the page another name, "Carlos."

The name Cerruti had some resonance with Rosacher, but though he racked his brain, he could not recall where he had heard it; and then, as he was settling in for an afternoon nap, he remembered Jarvis telling him about a scalehunter who lived on the plain near the dragon's hind leg. The man had gone by the nickname of Oddboy, this due to his eccentricity. He preferred the company of animals to that of men, and so had constructed a thatch-roofed house on the plain where he dwelled alone except for a menagerie of pets, all creatures peculiar to Griaule. Rosacher had never met the man and had not expected to, since Oddboy was a confirmed recluse, but he seemed to recall that his surname was Cerruti. Chances were, the scalehunter was not the same Cerruti, but it wasn't a common name in the region and Rosacher thought it might be worth a day's expedition to see whether or not he could be found.

Come morning, showered and, for the first time in weeks, clean shaven, armed with a hunting rifle, General Aldo's notebook and a pair of binoculars, he set forth on horseback, riding a bay gelding belonging to the House. He skirted Griaule's fearsome mouth and passed onto the plain, keeping his distance from the dark green cliff of the dragon's side, its true contours obscured at the base by mounded earth and grass, and higher up by vines and moss and epiphytes, most of the blooms pale lavender in color, but some few a lurid reddish orange that stood out from their surround like points of flame. His expectations of locating Cerruti were not high, yet as he rode his mood grew less oppressive. Though it was not yet nine o'clock, the sun was a dynamited white glare that cooked a strong scent from the stands of palmetto and broke a sweat on his back and shoulders. He went slowly, stopping now and again to scan the plain with his binoculars. When he drew near the haunch, he searched the landscape more carefully, but saw no house. Oddboy had likely moved on, but Rosacher wanted to be thorough and it was good to be out in the air after such a lengthy sequestration—he decided to continue searching. By mid-day he had traveled the length of the dragon, arriving at a place where the tail was completely buried beneath earth and grass, and there he tethered the bay and made a lunch of cold pork and grapes. It had been years since he'd ventured out on the plain and he had forgotten how extensive it was. Due to the clarity of the air, the low hills that encircled the valley appeared close at hand, yet he doubted he could reach them before nightfall. A fitful breeze stirred the tall yellow grasses, occasionally blowing with sufficient force to lift a palmetto frond, but otherwise everything was still—but it was an ominous stillness. The air seemed to hold a rapid vibration, the sum of the thousand heartbeats of the predators, great and small, that watched him from hiding. While digesting his lunch, he peered through the binoculars, tracking across thorn trees, acacias, more palmettos, shrimp plants, and then was brought up short by the sight of a pair of legs clad in coarse, dirty cloth. Dropping the binoculars, he scrambled to his feet. A man stood barely ten yards away—he was tanned, lean, with brown hair falling to his shoulders, and was shirtless, wearing sandals and a pair of ill-used canvas trousers. In one hand was a game sack figured by reddish-brown stains, and in the other a long-bladed knife. Before Rosacher could react, the man closed the distance between them. He was not so young as Rosacher had thought. Gray threaded his hair and deep lines scored his face, which had not been a pretty sight to begin with—long and horsey, with a hooked nose and squinty blue eyes, the schlera displaying a faint yellowish tinge. The nose had been broken more than once, and a ridged scar ran from the corner of his left eye and down onto his neck. His mouth worked as if he were trying to rid himself of a bad taste, and when he spoke it was in a nasal twang that was pitched an octave higher than Rosacher had anticipated.

"Man could get himself killed out here," he said. "You after getting killed?"

"No, I'm...I'm looking for someone."

"Must be someone real important, because you're taking one hell of a risk." The man's mouth worked again. "You're that Rosacher, ain't you?"

"You know me?"

"Seen you around. How'd you get your face fixed? Once a man gets burnt by flakes, he generally stays burnt."

"I'm not sure," Rosacher said. "It may be...it's difficult to explain."

The man grunted. "I suppose it is." He waved at the plain with his knife. "I was you, I wouldn't stay out here much longer. Something's liable to bite you in half."

He started to walk away, but Rosacher said, "Wait! I need to speak to Bruno Cerruti."

The man turned. "What for?"

"Are you Cerruti?"

"Ain't much point denying it. What you want?"

"Did a man named Aldo visit you recently."

"Man was out here a few weeks ago with some soldiers. Don't recall his name, but those soldiers scared the hell out of Frederick. It was a chore holding him back."

Rosacher didn't understand the reference to Frederick, but let it pass, sensing from Cerruti's truculent manner and clipped speech that he had a limited amount of time in which to make his inquiries and state his business. "What did Aldo want with you?"

"That's between me and him."

Sweat rolled down Rosacher's back, beaded on his forehead. "That's no longer the case. Aldo's dead."

"Huh. Too bad. Seemed like a nice little fellow." Cerruti spat out a brown wad of, Rosacher assumed, tobacco. "He was right took by Frederick. Said he had somebody needed killing. But the soldiers got Frederick excited and I advised him to leave. He said he'd come back later and we'd finish discussing the matter."

Rosacher wiped sweat from his eyes. "Is there someplace out of this heat where we can talk?"

Cerruti hesitated. "Guess we can head over to the house, but you best leave your animal here. Frederick loves horse meat."

✠

CERRUTI'S HOUSE WAS several hundred yards out onto the plain—it was almost impossible to see until you were close upon it, because its walls were woven of yellow grass, hardened (Cerruti said) by a paste derived from animal fat, and the roof was fabricated of palmetto fronds. The interior of the place held a rank odor and consisted of two large, windowless rooms separated by a canvas cloth; a second structure lay behind the house, nearly twice as high and missing a fourth wall—a storeroom, Rosacher supposed, yet he could see nothing within it, only blackness. It was not significantly cooler inside the house, but it was out of the direct sun. In the air was the sickly sweetish odor of a body that had gone unwashed for many days. Crudely carpentered chairs and a table of unfinished planking centered the room. Light came through chinks in the grass that had been made opaque by the paste and cast an irregular diamond pattern over the dirt floor.

"I was told you lived near the haunch." Rosacher took a chair and mopped his brow.

"Moved," Cerruti said.

He placed a jug and a platter bearing a dubious-looking chunk of fatty meat and a half-loaf of bread on the table and joined Rosacher. He nudged the plate toward Rosacher and nodded, indicating that he should help himself.

"I've already eaten." Rosacher shifted his chair forward. "What more can you tell me about your meeting with Aldo?"

"Wasn't much to it." Cerruti ripped a hunk of bread from the loaf. "He said he had somebody needed killing.

LUCIUS SHEPARD

Some high muckety-muck. Asked if me and Frederick would be interested in handling the job. I told him I didn't see no reason for it, so unless he told me more, he might as well head on back where he come from. That's when the soldiers started getting on Frederick's nerves."

"Where is Frederick?"

"Sleeping. He hates the sun, he does. Don't hardly ever come out until evening."

Cerruti tore off some of the meat with his teeth and chewed.

"Did he mention who this person was?" Rosacher asked.

"No. Just said he was a bigwig."

While Cerruti ate Rosacher studied Aldo's notebook, the page on which Cerruti's name had been written, along with "the hunt" and "Carlos." He remained baffled, unable to make a connection between Cerruti and those two entries.

Cerruti wiped his mouth on the back of his hand. "One thing I forgot. He said we'd have to travel a week and a day more to get to the place where the killing would be done."

Another useless fact—that was Rosacher's immediate response to this revelation; but as he tried to plot how far in every direction "a week and a day more" would take him (assuming the trip was made on horseback), he realized if he were to travel north and east that would put him within the Temalaguan border, on the edge of the rain forest, the area where Carlos VII, Temalagua's current ruler, famously pursued his passion for the hunt.

"Was the man he wanted killed named Carlos?" Rosacher asked.

Cerruti answered with his mouth full, shreds of meat falling onto the table. "Didn't say."

Had Aldo planned to assassinate the Temalaguan king? Was this his idea of a distraction that would delay an attack by the combined forces of Mospiel and Temalagua? It still made no sense to Rosacher. An ordinary death might cause the day-to-day routines of government to be pushed aside, giving way to the extensive planning and traditional pomp that attended Temalaguan state funerals, and the subsequent period of national mourning; but a political assassination would have the opposite effect, acting to spur on the new king in seeking vengeance. To have the desired effect, the assassination would have to be disguised as something else and, since Carlos would be protected by a sizeable armed guard, Rosacher was unable to fathom how this could be achieved.

He inquired further of Cerruti, but learned nothing more of value and, in order to prolong the conversation, he began asking irrelevant questions, hoping that stalling would give him time to think of something pertinent. Accordingly, one of the questions he asked was, "What happened to your menagerie of pets? I was told you had quite a collection."

"They didn't take to Frederick being around," said Cerruti. "Most of them run off."

This led Rosacher to think that he at least ought to wait for Frederick to wake up before returning to the House—he might have some intelligence to impart—and asked Cerruti how much longer Frederick could be expected to sleep.

"He'll be up and about by twilight," Cerruti said. "He enjoys hunting when it's cool."

Rosacher looked to the canvas curtain, behind which he presumed Frederick was sleeping, and was tempted to raise a clatter, a noise of some kind, sufficient to rouse him; but he decided that course of action would not be politic and asked Cerruti if he could wait there until Frederick awoke.

"You'd be putting your horse at risk." Cerruti chewed, swallowed. "I reckon leaving him out there until night, you're not going to find nothing but bones and the head. But if you're willing, it's all right with me."

Thankfully, because of Cerruti's laconic style, Rosacher did not feel it necessary to make conversation and, while his host busied himself with household chores, he tried to work on a plan of attack against Mospiel, given that Temalagua's involvement could be circumvented. The heat, however, overwhelmed him and he nodded off, drowsing through the long afternoon. He woke late in the day, about five o'clock judging by the rich golden light, and was clearing away the cobwebs, considering how to pass the hours before dusk, when he heard, from near at hand, a vast animal rumbling that raised the hair on the back of his neck. He jumped up from the chair, fumbled for his rifle, and said, "What in God's name is that?"

Cerruti sat opposite him, sharpening his knife on a whetstone—in the dim light, his hair half-obscuring his face, he seemed for the moment a wildly romantic figure and not an uneducated yokel. "Don't get all lathered up," he said. "That's just Frederick having a dream."

Rosacher let this sink in. "I thought Frederick was a man."

"He is. 'Least he says he is. You can make up your own mind."

Warily, Rosacher took his seat, but did not fall back asleep, his mind racing, alert to every noise. At twilight there came a renewed rumbling from without, louder and more extensive than before, and the sound of something big moving through the grass. Once again Rosacher shot to his feet and caught up his rifle.

"Easy, man!" Cerruti put a hand on his arm to restrain him. "Frederick don't care for rifles much, so you'd do well to leave it here."

Full of trepidation, Rosacher followed him out onto the plain, but saw nothing of Frederick. After the staleness of the house, the air felt fresh and cool. The sun was down behind Griaule's mountainous body and, except for a faint redness in the west, the plain was immersed in a purplish gloom, resembling in that crepuscular light pictures of the African veldt in books that Rosacher had thought exotic as a child, yet now seemed, in conjunction with the scene before him, to prefigure some occult menace.

He scanned the plain, searching for any object or movement that might signal Frederick's presence and saw in the distance a great dark shape flowing through the high grass, going very fast, much faster than a creature of its apparent size should be capable. It was speed without apparent purpose—the thing ran back and forth, and then in loops and circles, describing a variety of patterns that remained visible thanks to the flattened grass in its wake. Rosacher recognized that there was something playful about its exercise, like the running of a young dog that has been pent up for a while.

"You're a lucky man," Cerruti said. "Frederick's in a good mood. There's times he's right intolerant of strangers."

"That's Frederick?" said Rosacher, pointing at the dark shape, hoping for a negative response.

"In the flesh." Cerruti made a choking noise that might have been a laugh. "So to speak."

Rosacher wondered at the cause of Cerruti's amusement, but was so mesmerized by Frederick's to-and-fro dashes across the plain that he failed to inquire further. "I'll bring him over," Cerruti said. He did not call out or whistle or wave, yet Frederick abruptly changed course and came toward them at a good clip, growing in the space of three or four seconds from a dark shape a hundred yards away to a black featureless mound half the size of a full-grown elephant that settled in the grass a mere twenty feet away. Rosacher stumbled backward, terrified by the thing, by the chuffing of its breath, loud as a steam engine, and by its size and unstable surface—its substance, the stuff of its body, appeared to be in constant flux, a glossy black like polished onyx flowing across who-knows-what sort of structure, be it only more of the same blackness or a skeleton of sorts or something else, something completely implausible. It put Rosacher in mind of those oddments occasionally thrown up by the sea, a glob of protoplasm, a relic of some obscure life unknown and perhaps unknowable to man, a shapeless fragment broken or bitten off from a greater shapelessness...and yet as its breathing subsided, reduced to the level of a smithy's bellows, it seemed to flirt with a shape, to verge upon the animal, to assume for a fleeting instant the curves and musculature of an enormous sloth, or a bear with an elongated head and snout, and acquiring, too, a gamey odor that waxed and waned in accordance with the degree to which that shape was realized. Rosacher trembled before this monster, understanding death was near, but Cerruti, calm as ever, said, "Frederick wanted to know if that's your horse out there by the tail. I told him not to eat it."

Rosacher had neither heard nor seen any exhange between Cerruti and Frederick. In a shaky voice, he asked how they had communicated.

"I been hearing his voice in here..." Cerruti tapped the side of his head. "Ever since we met, maybe even before. Seems to me now like his voice was what led me to go back in under Griaule's wing in the first place. I'm right sure Frederick had it in mind to make me his dinner, but when he found out I could hear him and he could hear me, well, I guess you could say we became friends."

With a heavy exhalation, Frederick looked to sink lower into the grass, losing all hint of animal form, becoming as unstirring as a heap of dirt.

"This is the thing that lived under the wing?" Rosacher asked. "The thing everyone's been frightened of for so long?"

Frederick rumbled and Cerruti said, "He don't like you referring to him as a 'thing'."

"He understands me?"

Cerruti nodded. "Sure does. But to answer your question, way Frederick tells it, he was a man what lived around these parts back when folks were beginning to populate the valley. He worked the land, had a wife and children, but his true passion was for young girls, girls that had just bloomed. Thirteen, fourteen years old. Now and then he'd snap one up and take her in under the wing and do whatver he wanted. He must have done for a dozen or thereabouts. Came a day when one of the girls slipped away from him before he could drag her under the wing. She told her family what happened and they spread the word, and soon there was a whole mob searching for Frederick. He hid out under the wing, back in deep to where this kind of glowing moss lit up the space he was in, and there he stayed. Sometimes he'd sneak out at night to look for food, but he started losing his appetite and soon he hardly ever went out. And then he fell asleep. Wasn't no ordinary sleep. Frederick says that while he slept he could feel his body changing—he could feel his bones splintering, his organs dissolving. He felt every ounce of pain it took to make him into what he is now. How long it lasted, I can't say—but it was long. When he woke the pain was gone, but he was mad from the memory of it and he lashed out at people. Must have killed dozens...and that's when the legend got started. People forgot about Frederick and took to believing that there was a dangerous creature living back under the wing. Of course by then Frederick had lost his taste for people and turned to killing animals."

Rosacher masked his disgust for this murderer of young women, this once-human monster now become a monster in every sense of the word, and forced his attention to the problem at hand, thinking that if assassinating Carlos had been Aldo's intention, Frederick might well be the proper tool.

"Frederick," he said. "You can eat my horse."

The black mound quivered and swelled in volume to half-again its previous size.

"You sure about that?" Cerruti asked. "How are you going to get back?"

"I'll wait until morning and walk if needs be." Rosacher waved in the general direction of his horse. "Go ahead, Frederick."

The blackness swelled even more, nearly assuming an observable shape—giant sloth, bear, something along those lines—and flowed away toward the dragon's tail. Moments later, the horse screamed, a scream of fear that evolved into one of agony, and then was cut short.

Cerruti gave him an incurious look. "Why'd you do that?"

"I want to learn if the cadaver displays the type of wounds that result from an animal attack."

"You just wasted a good horse, then. You could have asked me. That horse is going to look like it was tore apart by lions." Cerruti spat. "Why you want to know that?"

"To find out if Frederick could kill the king of Temalagua and make it seem as though an animal had done it."

"What good's that going to do you? Frederick ain't killing no one without I say so. He's sure not going to be killing no king."

A SPRINKLING OF stars pricked the indigo expanse above Griaule's back and a cooling breeze came out of the north, drying the sweat on Rosacher's face. He felt suddenly confident that Aldo's intention had been to arrange the assassination of Carlos, and certain, too, that he would divine the next phase of Aldo's plan...or that he could create a plan equally as effective. He had come to rely on moments of illumination like this, perceiving them as sendings from the dragon, but in this instance, with the fate of the nation in the balance, an apprehension of his foolishness, of the ludicrous posture of faith, undercut his confidence. Still, he had little choice but to trust his instincts.

"Let's go and see how Frederick is faring," said Rosacher.

"I told you, ain't no point," said Cerruti. "Anyway, Frederick likes a little peace and quiet when he's eating. He won't be done for a while yet."

"Then let's wait a while and walk over there. Assuming they survived Frederick's assault, and I think they should have, I packed them quite carefully...I have several bottles of good red wine in my saddlebags. You and I can discuss things over a glass or two."

Cerrutti beamed. "Now I'm your man where wine is concerned."

"I knew you would be," Rosacher said.

14

UPON RETURNING TO THE House, Rosacher busied himself with scheming, studying Aldo's maps and charts, hoping to construct a strategy for blunting a potential aggression on the part of Mospiel. He made some progress, but deciding that he needed help with the plan, he met the following morning with Breque in the conference room where he had initially proposed an alliance between himself and the council. Also in attendance was Gerald Makdessi, a young colonel who had been on Aldo's staff and was thought to be a natural successor to the fallen general. He was a tall, punctilious man in his thirties, his close-cropped brown hair beginning to show gray, with a lean face that might have been laid out by a carpenter rule, its features were so standard—straight nose, thin, wide mouth, narrow blue-gray eyes all gathered within a tanned oblong frame. His expression—one of calm, attentive reserve—rarely changed, and then only by degree. As the men sat at the long mahogany table, their voices echoing slightly in the spacious room, the sun shafting through the eastern windows, its beams articulated by motes of glowing dust, Makdessi's movements were economical, confined to a slight inclination of the head, a gesture with the fingers, and the like. Once Rosacher had finished his presentation, he asked permission to speak.

"The morale of Mospiel's army is, as you have stated, not high," he said. "Their discipline is poor and I have been informed that there are influential elements within the command that differ with the prelates on the value of a war with Teocinte. They have no great will to fight, but they nonetheless present a formidable foe due to their sheer numbers. I recommend that we flood the garrison towns along the border with mab. And I recommend we do so immediately."

"Mospiel has made it clear that they would consider any attempt to introduce mab into their territory an act of war," said Breque.

"Yet they have permitted a black market in the drug to go more-or-less unchecked," Makdessi said. "Frankly, I doubt that they would notice the influx of drugs for several weeks, but even if they did, they can prepare for war no more quickly than they are at present. A sudden infusion of a drug that makes self-sacrifice less appealing, that lessens aggression and creates a lack of rigor in their preparation…it can't help but benefit our cause." He turned to Rosacher. "As to the city of Mospiel itself, your design is sound as far as it goes, but I have some ideas that may augment your own."

"Please, proceed," said Rosacher.

"In my view we should act boldly. We cannot afford to wait to learn if your attempt to assassinate Carlos has succeeded before initiating our attack on Mospiel." Makdessi cleared away papers from a map of the region and pointed to an area on the northern border. "Mospiel has always felt that the swamps of the Gran Chaco were a barrier against an attack from the north—and they would, indeed, negate the possibility of an army moving upon the city from that direction. But a force comprised of small independent units trained to negotiate that terrain, expert in hand-to-hand combat, a guerilla troop, if you will…that is a wholly different matter. Three years ago General Aldo and I, with the approval of the council, established such a force in the towns along the perimeter of the swamp. We have over eight hundred men and women in eleven separate communities who are often away from home for weeks at a time, engaged in trapping, trading, and other pursuits. Their absence from their homes will not be seen as extraordinary and thus will not be reported on by the operatives of the prelates. We should send this force into Mospiel as soon as possible."

"Why haven't I been told about this before?" Rosacher asked, the restraints on his temper starting to slip.

"I saw no great urgency to inform you," said Breque. "You were preoccupied with other matters... as was I."

"I was not so preoccupied that I wished to remain ignorant of a possible incursion into Mospiel."

"I was engaged on several fronts at the time, and thus I didn't think to notify you of the disposition of every matter. Perhaps I should in the future inform you of every shipment of toilet tissue, every..."

"An act of aggression against Mospiel is scarcely something so insignificant!"

"Gentlemen!" said Makdessi. "This is neither the time nor the place for such an unproductive digression. The situation is grave and I, at least, have duties to perform."

Rosacher shot a scathing look at Breque and waved in assent, and Breque said, "This is a trying time. Colonel. My apologies."

"At the same time we push in from the Gran Chaco," Makdessi went on, "we'll pull troops away from the Temalaguan border and march them toward our southern border with Mospiel, a point from which they might logically expect an attack to be launched. And then we strike with our elite cavalry unit farther north, the garrison at Ciudad Flores, with the aim of killing General Teixera and as many of his staff as we can." He leaned back from the map. "Teixera and his staff constitute the best of their military minds. If we're able to inflict casualties amongst them, we'll be well ahead of the game."

"I don't understand the purpose of your guerillas in the Gran Chaco." Rosacher said. "To what end will they be deployed?"

"They will endeavor to occupy the seat of power in Mospiel," Breque said. "The Temple of the Gentle Beast. That has been their goal from the outset. To occupy the temple and hold the hierarchy hostage."

"You intend to take the temple with only eight hundred men?" Rosacher shook his head in disbelief.

"I'll coordinate the attack myself." Makdessi said. "The Temple Guard are excellent soldiers, but so are we, and we will enter the complex disguised as pilgrims. The element of surprise will be ours. Once the temple is secured, it would take an army to dislodge us, and to do so would forfeit the lives of His High Holiness and the prelates."

"There are too many moving parts to this plan for my liking," said Rosacher.

Makdessi said, "We're in a desperate position. One that calls for desperate measures. We're bound to take a great many casualties—of that there is little doubt. But the virtue of this plan is that it doesn't require precise coordination between the various moving parts, as you put it. So long as they occur within a few days of each other, we have a decent chance of success."

"We'd be leaving Teocinte unprotected," said Breque. "If they were to launch a counter-offensive, it would be unopposed."

"The circumstance in which we find ourselves necessitates a certain amount of risk," said Makdessi. "There is no certain way to accomplish our aims, and to be conservative at this juncture would be to guarantee failure."

"In for a penny, in for a pound," said Rosacher.

"Precisely."

After a silence Breque said, "I think it would be best, Colonel, if you gave us an hour or two to discuss the situation. You may rest assured that we will give due consideration to all your recommendations."

When the door closed behind Colonel Makdessi, he said, "What do you think?"

"I'd watch that one if I were you," said Rosacher. "His ambition is likely aimed higher than the rank of general."

"My chief concern at the moment bears upon the question of whether he's capable of being a general. I'll worry about his ambition later."

"His plan seems reasonable given the circumstances."

"Did you think so?" Breque rubbed his cheek with his thumb. "I'm not sure."

The councilman's calm demeanor, the casual way he seemingly glossed over his duplicity, pricked Rosacher's anger again. "Is there anything else you have omitted telling me? Anything I should know before we decide this matter?"

"Damn it, Richard!" Breque spanked the table. "I apologize. It was an oversight for which I…"

"Oh, I very much doubt it was an oversight," said Rosacher. "You concealed from me the existence of a force whose primary function was to attack Mospiel. I wouldn't be surprised if you had engineered the entire situation, risked thousands of lives, just to fulfill your dreams of glory."

"You're one to talk about engineering situations!" Breque said, and would have said more, but Rosacher outvoiced him.

"I can see it now! Statues everywhere! Portraits, busts of Breque the Conqueror! Breque the Deliverer! Breque the All-Powerful!"

"Before this degenerates…"

"Who knows? Maybe even Saint Breque. Little schoolchildren will sing of your generosity and caring."

Breque, red-faced, mastered himself and said in a strained voice, "Before this degenerates into a shouting match, let me remind you that we have a decision to make. We need to set aside personal differences and act in accordance with our best judgment."

Rosacher bit back his response and sat glowering at Breque.

"I would like to hear more about this monster of yours," said Breque stiffly. "Do you really believe it's the same creature that lived for centuries beneath the wing?"

"What I believe has no bearing on its capacity for killing," said Rosacher. "But I have no reason to doubt the story. Nor would you, if you had seen it."

"It's made of a gelatinous substance, you say?"

"I said it appeared gelatinous, but I could just as easily say it appeared to be made of obsidian. What passes for its flesh is mutable in form and density. Once it seemed about to assume a fully defined shape, but..." Rosacher absently pushed papers around. "It is one of Griaule's creatures and thus we cannot hope to comprehend it. All you need to know is that it literally ripped my horse in half and that its speed is incredible. In the confined spaces offered by the jungle, Carlos and his men won't be able to stand against it."

"Interesting," said Breque. "That Griaule would choose such a flawed man to be his agent. That is, if Cerruti's story is true."

"All men are flawed."

"Yes, but not as terribly as this one."

"It strikes me that Griaule is adept at selecting the right man for the job. A deviant, a murderer...he becomes Griaule's guard dog. I assume that was Frederick's position before he became Cerruti's pet. And I'm certain Griaule saw some quality in you that, when nourished, would make you an efficient bureaucrat."

"That's a horrid compliment!" Breque punctuated the sentence with a barking laugh. "Of course it goes without saying that he must have seen something similar in you."

Rosacher shrugged.

"How much did you offer Cerruti?" Breque asked.

"Five thousand and free lodging at the House whenever he desires it."

"So little?"

"And a hundred horses for Frederick."

"I would have thought he'd ask for more."

"I told him that if Mospiel succeeded in their aggression, they would expand into the plain and make life difficult for him and Frederick. That engaged his patriotism." Rosacher placed his hands flat on the table, as though preparing to stand. "If there's nothing else, I have much to do before I depart."

"We haven't even begun our discussion of Makdessi's plan," said Breque.

"What is there to discuss? Every element of the plan works together in a way that promises the hope of success. A slim hope, perhaps, yet we can expect no more."

"But he's leaving the city undefended!"

Rosacher got to his feet. "The sole difference between Makdessi's plan and a plan that leaves a force to defend Teocinte is that, in the second instance, there will be more bodies piled up below Haver's Roost and our own attack will be commensurately less efficient. You know that as well as I."

"So you're comfortable with the rest of his design?"

"We might be able to put together a better plan, but how long would that take? How many opinions would we have to seek, how many consultations would we need to validate our conclusion? We cannot afford to mistrust our instincts. You've told me that Makdessi is the best available man to lead our troops. Very well. Let him lead."

"Of course you're right," Breque said after a pause, and sighed. "You'll be leaving in the morning?"

"Tonight, if possible. I've sent riders on ahead to spread rumors of a dangerous beast terrorizing a specific area of the jungle not far from the palace. I hope that by the time we reach that area, Carlos' interest will have been engaged, so that when Frederick's attacks begin, he'll be primed to come after him."

Breque nodded. "Good."

The councilman's tone of voice was dispirited, but Rosacher was in no mood to buck him up. "One more thing," he said. "We have a sufficient stock of mab to survive a two week lapse in production. I should be able to return by then. But if I do not..."

"We'll be fine as far as production goes no matter when you return."

"How can that be...unless you have succeeded in spying upon me and secured a knowledge of my process?"

"There is no process," said Breque. "I've been aware of that for years."

Rosacher sat back down.

"Ludie told me," Breque continued. "She yielded all your secrets before she died. She was not your friend... certainly not at the end."

Breque appeared to take no pleasure in this revelation—his glum countenance did not reflect the slightest joy or satisfaction.

"If that is so," Rosacher said, "why tell me? Why am I alive?"

"Why am I telling you?" Breque shook his head, as if bewildered by the question. "There was a time when I longed to tell you, when I wanted you to know who really was the master of our mutual circumstance. I wanted to tell you that day when I informed you of Ludie's death, but chose not to because I felt you would be easier to manage if you believed you were in control. But how I felt at that time is irrelevant. As I've told you, I've come to recognize your value as a resource and a friend."

"How could you ever perceive us to be friends? You've lied to me for decades."

"I understand that is how you see things, but though I had little respect for you in the past, and less love, my lie became a benign form of duplicity, a means of preserving the friendship. Your lies, on the other hand, have been funded, without exception, by your self-interest."

"Is this confession intended to persuade me to lower my guard where you're concerned? If so, I must tell you it has achieved the opposite effect."

Breque gestured to the heavens—he might have been importuning a deity. "I've always thought of myself as a ruthless politician, a skilled manipulator. Now that we are both facing the possibility of death,

I felt that honesty might prove a comfort to us both. As I've grown older, I've softened my stance, but even in my salad days, I could never match you as regards ruthlessness and manipulation. You are relentless in the practice of those arts. Perhaps the fact that you don't appear to have aged...perhaps it is not merely appearance. That might explain why you have failed to grow more understanding of other men's frailties." He stood. "At any rate, there it is. You have regained the advantage over me. I have no cards left to play."

"I realize that is what you wish me to think," Rosacher said. "But I would not be the man you judge me to be if I accepted your statement as fact."

Breque threw up his hands. "Think what you want! I'm done with this discussion."

"We'll talk further upon my return," said Rosacher—despite himself, he felt badly for Breque.

"I'm certain you will return," Breque said. "Griaule is clearly your protector. But is he mine? That remains to be seen."

THOUGH THEY BEGAN their journey at night, Cerruti and Rosacher thereafter traveled by day, leaving Frederick to follow their scent. The days passed without significant event. At night, Rosacher could hear Frederick moving out in the brush, beyond the light of their campfire, and on those nights when he did not hear the beast, to ease his mind Cerruti would summon him and Frederick would materialize as a puddle of shadow or a heap of blackness, staying in sight just long enough to fray Rosacher's nerves.

The hours that proved the most onerous for Rosacher were those between dusk, when they pitched camp, and when they went to sleep. Simply put, Cerruti was a bore. He regaled Rosacher with stories about minor wounds he had suffered, tooth problems, illnesses he had endured, encounters with poisonous plants and pests such as fleas and lice, as well as afflictions of unknown origin. As he told it, his life had been spent in a condition of mild constant pain, and this was the only subject about which he was at all voluble. In opposition to his usual taciturn manner, he related his experiences with a kind of crude eloquence, describing his various injuries and symptoms in detail. He seemed to have relished each abrasion and cut, each festering sore and fever and runny nose. Everything they saw reminded him of some incidence of sickness or impairment, and whenever Rosacher tried to turn their campfire chats to a subject more to his pleasure, Cerruti would answer in a terse fashion and then go on with his litany of medical woes. Not even Frederick, a topic about which Rosacher thought that Cerruti would wish to display his expertise, warranted a detailed response. When asked to expound on Frederick's method of communication, the shape he preferred to assume, or any other facet of its behavior, Cerruti would provide an answer both brief and uninformative, leading Rosacher to suspect that he knew considerably less than he pretended and was glossing over his ignorance. He wondered, too, if Cerruti had as much control over Frederick as he claimed and whether or not, when the time came to unleash his pet, Cerruti would be able to reel it in.

They crossed over the Temalaguan border on the sixth day, passing into a region of dense jungle that impeded their progress and brought to Cerruti's narratives of illness a new level of intensity. They camped that evening near a bend in the Rio Coco beneath a canopy of aguacaste trees, on a patch of packed earth that had been cleared of vegetation by the passage of tapirs and various other animals—it had rained earlier in the day and their tracks pockmarked the moist clay. Ordinarily Rosacher would have chosen a different place in which to camp. It was obviously part of a trail leading to a watering hole and as such was sure to attract predators; but with Frederick lurking nearby and his rifle to hand, he felt secure. As dusk blended into full dark and the vine-hung canopy vanished from sight, he would have expected to hear the droning of insects and the liquid repetitions of frogs, but the only sounds he heard before falling asleep that night were those of Frederick's predation—a high, thin squeal cut short—and the crackling of their fire and the whining constancy of Cerruti's voice celebrating each new mosquito bite with a narrative of past travails.

"I was up on the coast a'ways once, not far from Buttermilk Key, traveling in a caravan," he said, slathering his arms with a pale yellow ointment that, he claimed, would drive off any six-legged creature. "That was the worst place I ever saw for bugs. When the wind off the water died, you could stick your arm out the window of the wagon and it'd turn black with mosquitoes in a second or two."

Rosacher was busy rubbing his exposed skin with water in which he had dissolved a number of small, black cigars. His method of repelling mosquitoes. "I wouldn't have stuck my arm out, then," he said.

"Had to, it was so damn hot. Not like here. Here, the heat's uncomfortable, but up on the coast the heat's pestilential." He repeated the word, as if enunciating it gave him satisfaction. "Anyhow, my bites got infected and my arm swole up the size of a hawser. They were draining pus from it for a week."

Rosacher lit one of the cigars and puffed out a cloud of smoke and said without the least emotional inflection, "That's awful."

"Too right it was! They must have took a gallon out of me."

"Speaking of bodily fluids and the like," said Rosacher. "Have you ever noticed whether Frederick defecates after eating?"

Cerruti, likely irritated by Rosacher's lack of interest in his arm, said, "Hell, no."

"We've been traveling with Frederick for a week and I haven't seen any sign of his spoor. Don't you find that odd, considering the fact that he's consumed half-a-dozen large animals…and that's only the ones we've run across?"

"Frederick's a fastidious type," Cerruti said. "He does his business in private."

Recalling the condition of the animal cadavers, Rosacher did not think the word "fastidious" would apply to any of Frederick's behaviors; but he let it pass. "I'd be interested in examining one of his stools. It might prove instructive in determining the workings of his digestive system."

Cerruti rubbed ointment into his neck. "Got better things to do than look for Frederick's shit."

"Could you ask him or me? I'm very interested in his physiological characteristics."

"You want to rile up Frederick, that's a good way to do it—asking about his private business. He don't like talking about it."

"What does he like talking about? I'm assuming that you and Frederick have had occasion to chat from time to time."

"He don't usually have much to say," said Cerruti. He stopped applying ointment and his body language displayed, Rosacher thought, a degree of wariness. "He tells me what's been hunting, for one thing. His conversation don't run too deep, if you catch my meaning."

"You're saying that you don't engage in philosophical speculations, that sort of thing?"

Cerruti peered across the fire at Rosacher, as if trying to read his face.

"Do you ever speak about old wounds and illnesses, as you do with me?" asked Rosacher.

"Oh, aye!" Cerruti brightened. "We swap stories all the time."

"I wouldn't think Frederick would be vulnerable to much."

Cerruti sat up straighter, eager to talk now that the subject was more to his liking. "Most of the time he's not, but there's times when he's prone to injury as you or me."

A night bird passed overhead, giving an ululating cry; the wind shifted, bringing a sweetish odor off the river to mix in with the dark green scents of the foliage.

"Really?" said Rosacher, not wishing to appear overly inquisitive, but thinking this might be an opportunity to learn something salient about Frederick.

"He's often injured when he's feeding. He gets so damn hungry, sometimes he fails to finish an animal off before he starts in and whatever it is he takes a bite of is liable to mark him with a claw or a tooth."

"Do they leave a scar?"

"Naw, you seen him. Whatever damage is done gets healed up when he pulls back from eating."

A host of questions occurred to Rosacher, but he left them unspoken for fear of making Cerruti uneasy.

"Pity we can't do the same," he said.

Cerruti looked perplexed, but then he grinned. "If we had a body for feeding and another for healing like Frederick, the law couldn't never touch us."

"I don't suppose it could."

Cerruti relaunched his tale of mosquitoes and pus, and Rosacher did not attempt to dissuade him. He lay back, responding to Cerruti's recitation of his maladies with grunts and other affirmations, trying to piece together the few things he knew about Frederick into a coherent picture, and soon drifted off to sleep.

In the morning, they followed the river course through a dense whitish mist that made every feathery frond, every loop of vine, into an article of menace. A pack of howler monkeys trailed them for a while, their cries seeming to issue from the throats of enormous beasts whose heads were thirty feet above the jungle floor. Sunlight thinned the mist and the poisonous greens and yellow-greens of the foliage emerged. Swarms of flies came to plague them, rising from mattes of vines beneath the hooves of their horses. Serpents could be seen swimming in the murky green water. The heat merged the dank scent of the river and that of a trillion tiny deaths with the great vegetable odor of the jungle, combining them into a cloying reek that so clotted Rosacher's nostrils, he did not think he ever again would be able to smell the slight fragrance of a flower or a woman's perfume.

In late afternoon they arrived at the village of Becan, on the edge of the king's hunting ground amidst banana trees and one towering mago tree whose ripening fruit hung from structures that looked as ornate as candlelabras—it was a dismal collection of huts constructed of sapling poles and thatch, its muddy streets dappled with puddles. At the center of the village was a longhouse where travelers were permitted to sleep in hammocks for the night, and close by the longhouse was a largish hut, overhung by the leaves of a banana tree, wherein a wizened, white-haired old man, dressed in clothes made from flour sacking, with perhaps a dozen teeth left in his head, sat behind an empty crate and dispensed cups of unrefined rum. The late sun shining through the poles striped the dirt floor. Four wooden tables were arranged about the interior, but only six chairs, one toppled on its side and another occupied by a young woman who might have been pretty had she run a brush through her tangled hair and washed away the grime from her face and worn something more appealing than loose canvas trousers and a blouse that was mostly rips and stains. She affected what Rosacher judged to be a seductive pose and smiled at the two men as they entered, thus advertising her function. With a palsied hand, the old man began to pour from a bottle half-full of yellowish liquid. Rosacher laid a hand over the cup the old man had provided, but Cerruti gulped down his measure and gave a satisfied sigh.

"Another?" the old man asked.

Cerruti looked to Rosacher, who nodded, and the old man proceeded to pour.

"Do you have anything else to drink?" Rosacher asked.

"Yes, but it's very expensive. Twelve quetzales for a small measure."

"Let's see it."

Cerruti pulled up a chair next to the woman and they spoke together in muted tones.

From the rear of the packing crate, the old man withdrew a bottle wrapped in a red cloth and displayed it: Scotch whiskey, a decent brand. Rosacher signaled him to pour and leaned against the crate, gazing through the door of the cantina. A rooster hurried past, clucking, pursued in short order by a naked toddler. At the rear of one of the huts, a matronly woman in a striped dress was taking down her wash. The old man made a production out of cleaning Rosacher's cup with a filthy rag and poured. As Rosacher drank, he asked if they had come from Teocinte.

"From Mospiel." Rosacher pushed his cup toward the old man, asking for a refill, and handed him a fifty quetzal note.

"I have no change," the old man said.

"I'll drink it up," said Rosacher, and the old man beamed.

Cerruti stood, linked arms with the woman and, with a salute to Rosacher, the two of them headed toward a hut on the far side of the longhouse.

"And what are you doing in Temalagua?" asked the old man.

"I am a trader in exotic birds. I'm going to the market in Alta Miron to buy stock." Rosacher sipped the whiskey. "Truly, I did not think I would ever come to Alta Miron. Last night we were attacked in our camp by a beast. We were lucky to survive."

"What manner of beast?"

"I did not get a good look at it. But it was black and very large. It trampled the jungle flat around our campsite. We eluded it by diving into the river. It killed one of our horses."

The old man attempted a whistle in appreciation of Rosacher's story, but due to his lack of teeth all that emerged was a breathy sound. "I have heard of this beast," he said. "It's said it killed a mother and her daughter in Dulce Nombre."

"What a pity!" Rosacher said, chalking up the story to the rumors started by the riders he had sent on ahead and the typical hyperbole of Temalaguan storytellers.

"Indeed! But there is good news. It is said King Carlos will hunt the beast. Some of the men from our village have gone to the capital to volunteer their services."

"Why would Carlos look to Becan for help? I'm certain his guards can ably assist him."

"The men of Becan are accomplished trackers," said the old man pridefully. "We have assisted the king on other hunts. And Carlos is a friend to the village. In fact it was he who presented me with this bottle"—he indicated the whiskey—"so he might have something suitable to drink when he stops by."

"If that's the case, should you be selling me whiskey?"

"Carlos is generous and kind. All I needs do is tell him I've run out and he sends me a new bottle."

"Then I'll have another."

Darkness slipped in, lamps were lit in the little huts, their gapped walls revealing families moving about within and the jungle resounded with the singing of insects and frogs. The old man, whose name was Alonso, served a dinner of beans and rice and chorizo, brought by a sallow girl with a cast in one eye. He joined Rosacher at a table and told stories of the village and the king. How Carlos had shot the man-eating jaguar of Saxache, a creature that, once dead, had turned back into an elderly woman, a bruja of some reknown. How Carlos had hunted down the great caiman of El Tamarindo, also a killer of men—its head was now mounted above the Onyx Throne. How Carlos had brought doctors and medicine to Becan when the village had been afflicted with dysentery. Other men dropped by and, after being introduced to Rosacher, joined he and Alonso for a drink. They, too, spoke highly of the king's courage and largesse, and one, a bearded fellow by the name of Refugio, missing a leg, told of how Carlos, his rifle empty, armed only with a machete, had risked his life to save him from a wild boar.

"A man like that," Refugio said. "A rich and power-ful man who would sacrifice his life for someone poor like me when he has so much to live for...he is much more than a king. He has been crowned by the gods and will one day reign with the Beast in heaven."

"Truly," said Alonso, and the other men echoed his sentiments.

Tipsy now, sweating profusely in the windless night, in that cramped circle of men, Rosacher understood for the first time that he intended to kill a man who had done far more good than evil. Even if one discounted the stories as embellished, it was impossible to deny that Carlos was an anomaly, a benevolent ruler in a region that consistently spawned kings who were little more than human monsters with the souls of jackals. He tried to think of how to avoid killing Carlos, but made no headway and instead bought the house a round from another example of the king's largesse, a second and previously unopened bottle of Scotch. This accentuated the air of rough bonhomie that had come to govern the cantina, and soon stories about the king were replaced by songs that celebrated women, famous hunts, and the fictive events that masqueraded as glorious Temalaguan history. A choir of drunken voices served to suppress Rosacher's guilt, but not to drown it utterly. As a result he happily joined in the singing, but his joy was com-promised by an undercurrent of fretful thought and half-formed plans to return to Teocinte, his mission unfulfilled, and the possibility that he could approach Carlos, persuade him not to join forces with Mospiel. He entertained the notion that he was fighting on the wrong side and that he should immediately break with the city council, with Breque, the only member of the council who mattered, and throw his weight behind Mospiel and Temalagua.

He heard the screaming before he really registered it and, by the time he clutched for his rifle, it had ceased and all that could be heard was a snapping of poles and thatch crunching and the hoarse shouts of the men who had preceded him through the door of the cantina. He staggered out into the night and saw people running toward the ruins of a hut across the way. He followed them and then realized that the ruined hut was the same one toward which Cerruti and the woman had been heading.

He sprinted to the hut, thrust people aside, and saw Cerruti, naked, smeared with blood, sitting against the remnants of a wall, head in hands. Some of the thatch lay across the pallet where Cerruti and the woman had been, and was soaking in a puddle of dark arterial blood. Rosacher knelt and Cerruti glanced up, wild-eyed, strings of mucous hanging from his nose. He tried to speak, but only a bubble of spit came forth. The villagers behind Rosacher babbled and someone let out a wail.

"He plucked her right off me." Cerruti appeared to be speaking to someone hovering above his head. "I's

LUCIUS SHEPARD

giving her a ride and Frederick..." His breath caught in his throat and he started sobbing.

"Shh! It's all right!" Rosacher held his head, hoping to silence him before he gave away their part in this butchery.

"His face..." Cerruti's voice was partially muffled by Rosacher's chest. "I never seen Frederick like that before."

"Get a hold of yourself, man!" Rosacher pulled Cerruti more tightly to him and whispered in his ear, "People are listening!"

"He didn't act like he knew me!"

"Here! Help me with him," Rosacher said to the villagers. "Get him a blanket!"

As he walked Cerruti over to the cantina, Rosacher caught snatches of conversation: "What will Adelia do now? Yasmin was her sole support." "Give me something to wipe off the blood." "He said, 'Frederick'. Who is Frederick?" "Alonso, bring a cup of water!"

Once Cerruti was seated in the cantina, he grew unresponsive to questions and stared into space, his lips moving silently. Relieved to see this, yet concerned for his well-being, Rosacher helped to clean the blood away and forced him to drink a glass of rum. Several of the men talked about forming a party to go after Frederick and the woman, Yasmin, but Rosacher dissuaded them, relating his "experiences" of the previous night and telling them that the creature was too fast and powerful for them to go off half-cocked. The headman of the village dispatched a rider to Alta Miron so as to inform the king and Rosacher made no attempt to interfere with this. He had abandoned his misgivings about killing Carlos, feeling that the die was cast, and thought that if the king could be brought to Becan, it would not only make their task easier, it would be proof that Griaule's will was at work here.

After the furor had subsided and many anecdotes had been told about where this and that person was and what they had been doing when Yasmin was taken, Rosacher led Cerruti to the longhouse and helped him into a hammock. Though the night was humid, almost as warm as the day, Cerruti shivered and complained feebly of the cold. Clearly, he was in shock. Having no medicine, all Rosacher could do was keep him warm and talk to him. The headman had set guards with torches and machetes about the village in case Frederick returned, some of them standing watch beside the longhouse, and he was thus forced to keep his voice low, but he enjoined Cerruti to hang on, saying he needed him in order to direct Frederick, and finally managed to elicit some coherent responses.

"It's my fault for lying with her," said Cerruti at one point. "I wouldn't have done, if I'd thought Frederick was about."

His sweaty face, a pale orange in the dim, flickering light, was a mask of anxiety and anguish.

"He can't abide women around me," said Cerruti. "Or maybe it's just women and I got nothing to do with it."

Rosacher cautioned him once again to lower his voice. "Can you tell if he's still out there?"

"Oh, he's out there. He never goes far."

"Will he do the job for us? Can you still control him?"

Cerruti nodded, or it might have been a shiver. Rosacher asked the question again.

"He'll do your killing." Sweat beaded on Cerruti's brow. His skin was ghastly pale and the shadows in his eyes looked moist and feverish. "He'll do your killing and more, don't you worry."

CERRUTI'S FEVER ABATED during the night, his temperature went down and his heartbeat grew regular. He slept late in the morning and was able to eat a breakfast of tortillas, rice and beans in the cantina. The villagers had cleared away the wreckage of the hut, restoring a semblance of normalcy to their home. Chickens and pigs foraged in the dirt, grubby children sucked on mango pulp, and hobbled beside a banana tree, a donkey that Frederick had passed over in favor of Yasmin stood placidly, chewing on a stalk of sugar cane.

AFTER BREAKFAST, ROSACHER cautioned Cerruti against speaking about Frederick and retired to his hammock, hoping to sleep for an hour or two; but his mind was agitated and sleep would not come. Having to care for Cerruti had suppressed his anxieties and, relieved of that duty, he thought of all that could go wrong. He wondered if Frederick, as Alonso had suggested, had been responsible for the death of the mother and child in Dulce Nombre—it did not seem so implausible now. And what did that say about Cerruti's ability to control his pet? Rosacher suspected that Cerruti's control was subject to Frederick's inclination and doubted that the task before them could be accomplished with anything approaching ease. Would Frederick go after any woman who came close to Cerruti...and what if the king had women in his retinue, a distinct possibility. These and other related concerns pressed in on him until at last he sank under their weight and lapsed into a sleep troubled by dreams in which he lay awake, worrying about this and that.

A clamor of voices, of horses neighing and being steadied, woke him. He lay still for a minute or thereabouts, unable to bring these sounds into focus. His head throbbed and his heart fluttered. A few minutes more elapsed and he sat up. In front of the cantina were a group of brown-skinned men wearing royal livery, perhaps ten or twelve, and an equal number of horses. The villagers crowded around them, all speaking at once.

Rosacher swung his legs out of the hammock, blinking against the morning light, and went to the door. The man central to this hubbub was not in the least imposing: he had a pale complexion and was of average height, with neatly trimmed brown hair and a Vandyke. Handsome, but not remarkably so. Clad in a red doublet trimmed with gold and khaki riding trousers. Had it not been for the beard, which was meticulously barbered, a foppish accessory shaved into points along his jaw, Rosacher might not have recognized him; but recognize him he did. This very man had come to the House of Griaule not two years before, in the company of a half-dozen other men, seeking information about a young woman who had been employed there. A cousin, as Rosacher recalled. The man had traveled under an assumed name, but it was evident by the attentiveness of his retinue that this was Carlos. Stunned by the fact that he had previously had dealings with the king, Rosacher retreated into the shade of the longhouse, debating how best to handle the situation, whether to dissemble and hope that Carlos would not recognize him or to put on a bold face and own up to the fact that he and the king had met before. After smoothing down his hair, deciding to trust his instincts on how he should proceed, Rosacher walked out into the light and was quickly pushed forward into the king's presence by the villagers, who claimed him to be someone with intimate knowledge of the monster.

After making a salutatory bow, Rosacher thought he detected a flicker in the king's expression and, thinking that this signaled recognition on the king's part, he said, "It may be presumptuous of me, Your Majesty, but is it possible that we have met before?"

"Carlos," said the king. "There are no majesties here. Yes, I was thinking the same thing myself." He studied Rosacher for a moment. "The House of Griaule, was it not? You're the elusive Mister Mountroyal's aide de camp. I'm sorry...I've forgotten your name."

"Myree," said Rosacher. "Arthur Myree. I did serve Mister Mountroyal for a brief period in that capacity, but we parted ways after a disagreement over salary. I am now a trader in exotic birds."

"So Alonso tells me." Carlos indicated that Rosacher should enter the cantina. "I have spoken with your companion, Mister Cerruti, about the beast that attacked him, but he was not very forthcoming. I'm eager to hear what you have to tell me."

"Where is he?" Rosacher asked, as he stepped inside the cantina. "He was suffering from shock and may need medical attention."

"He's with another of my party. An artist. I hope he'll be able to describe what he saw and that my artist is able to capture its likeness. I'll have my doctor look in on him once he's done."

Alonso served Rosacher a plate of beans, rice and fried plantains. As he ate, he told Carlos the story he had earlier told Alonso and, when he had done, the king said, "It would appear that the creature is nocturnal. All the attacks thusfar have occurred at night...though one of the three killed in Dulce Nombre occurred near dawn."

"Three?" Rosacher set down his fork. "I was told only two, a mother and daughter."

"There were three. A girl sent to fetch water with which to prepare the morning meal. She happened upon the remains of the other two and was killed. A black shape was seen feeding upon her flesh, but the witness was too terrified to remember much detail."

The acuity that Carlos brought to bear on him as they talked unsettled Rosacher. The king seemed to register his every movement, every change in expression, but Rosacher maintained the demeanor of a man who had been through a frightening experience, yet had mastered himself and was trying to be helpful—he did so, he believed, without error, but he could not be certain as to what Carlos perceived.

Their conversation was interrupted by a middle-aged man whom Carlos introduced as Ramon, who brought with him a large sketchbook that he handed to Carlos. Rosacher asked Carlos, who was leafing through the sketchbook, if he was in the habit of traveling with an artist.

"I am a vain man in many ways," Carlos said. "Often I am unable to bring home a trophy from my hunts, and thus Ramon travels with me to record my successes and failures."

He stopped leafing through the book and showed Ramon one of the pages. "This?"

"He swore it was accurate," Ramon said. "But his memory may have produced an exaggerated image."

Carlos handed the book to Rosacher. On the page was the sketch of a furred animal standing on its hind legs, as might a bear, but with an elongated head that resolved into the leathery face of a horrid old man, so distorted and vile, every wrinkle and line etched so deeply that it appeared the face of a demon, its mouth open to reveal an array of needle-like teeth framed by fangs. The drawing was beautifully rendered and shaded, rife with delicate lines that implied musculature—in the manner of one of Durer's engravings. Rosacher gazed at it, struck speechless by this representation of, he assumed, Frederick's base form.

"There are a few details over here," Ramon volunteered, encouraging Rosacher to turn to the next page.

A black paw with three nasty-looking talons; an eye, almost human, but having a slit pupil and red shadings at the corners; a fang and several teeth, discolored in the way of ivory.

"Does any of this seem familiar?" Carlos asked.

Rosacher shook his head—he no longer had to act in order to simulate the confusion of the recently traumatized. "No, I...I never saw its face, but this...It's impossible! It's the face of something out of hell!" He laid down the sketchbook. "It can't be!"

"Cerruti swears to it," Ramon said.

"He was in shock! His memory can't be trusted."

"The only sure way to ascertain the truth," said Carlos, "is to hunt it down and kill it. I hope that you and Mister Cerruti will join us in the enterprise."

Confounded by this pronouncement, Rosacher fumbled for an excuse, citing fatigue and the need to be in Alta Miron by market day; but the king insisted, saying, "There will be other market days and I assure you that you will not find the hunt taxing. We will set a trap for the creature at some distance from the village, but not too far away, and near the river so that we're able to take refuge should the occasion arise."

"I fear for Mister Cerruti's health," said Rosacher. "Perhaps he should be left back to recuperate."

"My doctor will examine him and make a determination." Carlos laid his hands flat on the table. "In the meantime, my men will go on ahead to find a suitable location for a campsite. We will join them in mid-afternoon. You may do as you wish until then. Sleep, rest…or if you will grant me the pleasure of your company, we can chat some more. I'm sure both of us would find it edifying."

15

RY AS HE MIGHT, Rosacher could find no viable reason why Teocinte's national integrity should be preserved at the cost of Carlos' life. Aside from being vain about his appearance and his skill as a hunter, the king had no apparent flaws. Over the next few hours he discussed with Rosacher his intentions for the people of Temalagua, a grand design involving land reform and the gradual elevation of the peasant class by means of education and the opportunities presented by an emerging industrial state. He treated all around him as equals and they clearly loved him—not only the villagers, but also his guards, who engaged their king in rough yet good-natured repartee, and those who, upon hearing of the king's presence in Becan, had made their way to the village in order to pay their respects and, in some few instances, to ask that he decide some matter of local controversy—this he did with uncommon grace and charity. A case in point, Gregorio, a farmer from the town of Sayaxche whose wife had left him for another man—all three parties came before the king to offer testimony. Gregorio's wife, Bedelia, did not deny that Gregorio was a decent man and a good provider, but they had married sixteen years ago when they were but children and she had fallen out of love with him and in love with Camilio, who owned a dry goods store. Since her union with Gregorio had proven childless, and as she was already carrying Camilio's child, she felt justified in moving on with her life. Gregorio claimed to love Bedelia still and, though not a violent man by nature, he had been humiliated and was plagued by thoughts of retribution. For his part, Camilio wanted to avoid bloodshed, but did not believe this would be possible under the circumstances, since he was unwilling to foreswear his love for Bedelia and refused to relinquish his parental rights to the child. The king adjudicated the matter thusly: "In my palace there are many lovely women, the great majority of them yet unwed. I invite you, Gregorio, to come to Alta Miron and live on the palace grounds and work in my gardens, this in the hope you will find there a more suitable wife. If at the end of a year, you have not found a wife or are otherwise unhappy in your estate, you may return to Sayaxche."

Carlos then turned to Bedelia and Camilio. "You will see that Gregorio's fields are worked and worked well for the term of one year, with all profit going to Gregorio. Should he return to Sayaxche, the fields will revert to his ownership. Should he not return, the fields will become yours. As to the child, is his parentage in dispute?"

Gregorio lowered his eyes and said, "No."

"Then the child shall remain with Bedelia and Camilio," said Carlos. "But I hereby direct and declare that Gregorio be named the child's godfather. It is my hope that this shared responsibility will over time heal the breech between you." He turned again to Gregorio. "A condition attaches to my offer: you will leave within the hour for Alta Miron, thereby avoiding any further conflict with your wife and Camilio. I will give you a paper signed by my hand and sealed with my ring to present at the palace gates. You will be installed in your quarters and on the morrow you will begin what I trust will be a fruitful and happy life."

All parties appeared satisfied with this agreement, Camilio less so for having to take on the burden of working Gregorio's fields, but Bedelia expressed her contentment with the king's justice and it was evident from Gregorio's smile that he had overstated his love for Bedelia and would not be returning soon to Sayaxche, exhilarated by the potentials of life at the palace and a prospect of work far less onerous and better paid than that of a farmer.

Carlos' rendering of this judgment, the facility with which he had delivered it and the kindly yet firm manner of handling a ticklish situation made an impression on Rosacher. It reminded him of how he had come to deal with people, except that with his winning charm and patience, his clear intent to be even-handed in all things, Carlos seemed a better him, an idealized Rosacher, one who did not manipulate for gain but was motivated by the desire to govern fairly. The idea that he was about to kill such a man grew ever more unappetizing and Rosacher's guilt was amplified when the king invited him to the palace upon the conclusion of the hunt so that he could select from amongst the rare birds in the royal aviary a bird or two of his choosing, this in compensation for his assistance in trapping the beast that had terrorized the villages of Becan and Dulce Nombre.

"I believe our golden caiques have recently reproduced," said Carlos. "Perhaps you would consider one of their children a fitting reward."

"I would be honored by such a gift," said Rosacher.

In mid-afternoon they rode to the camp established by the king's guard on the banks of the Rio Coco. An area some forty feet in length and half that in width had been cleared about the king's tent, situated on the verge of the water. A table and chairs had been placed in front of the tent and it was here that Rosacher and Carlos seated themselves, attended by one of the guards who provided a meal of sandwiches, chicken and pork, and a good burgundy. Riflemen had been positioned here and there in the surrounding jungle, setting up a crossfire, and both Carlos and Rosacher kept their rifles at the ready. Cerruti sat on the ground at the edge of the jungle some thirty feet away, joined there by a group of men from Becan also armed with rifles. That he and Cerruti were being kept separate caused Rosacher a modicum of unease, but he told himself that this must be a question of class and, though it seemed out of character for Carlos to make such distinctions, he likely was bound by some personal regulation that prohibited his association with a ruffian of Cerruti's stamp...or it might be that during his interview with Cerruti, which had occurred while Rosacher slept, he had developed a distaste for the man and did not relish his company. The disquiet Rosacher felt in relation to this state of affairs gradually ebbed, washed away by Carlos' affable and diverting conversation, but his anxiety over Frederick and the murder of the king did not abate. Whenever possible, he tried to catch Cerruti's eye and, when he managed to do so, he gave his head a surreptitious shake, thereby hoping to communicate his desire to have Cerruti call off his pet and end their mission. Once he thought Cerruti responded with a minimal nod, but he could not be confident that this had been anything other than a twitch, since certain of Cerruti's behaviors—long stares into nowhere and a general unresponsiveness to the men about him— gave evidence that he remained traumatized. Rosacher reached a point in his mental process at which he recognized that he had done all that he could short of making a full confession to Carlos, an admission that would guarantee his execution, and realized that he had put his fate into Griaule's hands or, assuming the dragon's indifference, had left it to chance.

As dusk gave way to night, the lingering afterglow of the sun reduced to a ragged band of indigo at the edge of the world, torches were lit, lending an air of barbarity to the encampment. Insects sizzled, frogs bleeped and belched up deeper sounds, the river gurgled placidly, a night-blooming cereus yielded its soft perfume, and Rosacher drank most of a second bottle of wine, and not because he was desperate—he had bypassed desperation and gone straight to an acceptance of his lot. If this was to be all of life, so be it. He'd had enough of striving, of contending against the forces of man and nature (he was convinced that the two were hopelessly at odds), and he surrendered happily to the kingdom of wine, the nation of tipsiness, and whatever constituency those entities embodied. The night was exceptional in its clarity. Stars like wildfire orchids sparked in the overhanging boughs of the great trees and the color of the sky, a rich, deep blue, a royal blue, seemed the product of a curdled mass of light behind it, as if a small galaxy had been brought close to the earth but was held just out of view, so as to illuminate an intimate scene on the riverbank, a pocket of tranquility at the heart of a diseased and trembling world.

"Richard..." said Carlos. "May I call you Richard?"

Rosacher froze and before he could think of a clever lie, something that could extricate him from a circumstance he had only begun to comprehend, he realized that his reaction had already given him away—yet still he made the effort and said to the king, "I beg your pardon?"

"Are you aware, Mister Rosacher, that there is no such bird as a golden caique?" Carlos asked.

"I assumed you spoke out of ignorance," Rosacher said. "I didn't think it my place to correct you."

"I might believe you if you were not Richard Rosacher, but since you are..." Carlos made a comically sad face. "I don't?"

Rosacher rummaged about for an escape, some trick of words to persuade Carlos that he was not this Rosacher; but he had drunk too much and was too far gone along the road of surrender. "What are you going to do with me?" he asked.

"It's as I said. You'll be my guest at the palace."

"But what will be my punishment?"

"Why should I punish you? Have you committed some crime? True, you operate a business of which I disapprove, and you are the de facto representative of a government that has been no friend to Temalagua. And I suppose you and Mister Cerruti have entered the country illegally—but the penalty for that is a fine and expulsion from Temalaguan soil."

"Your predecessors have chosen to interpret 'expulsion from Temalaguan soil' rather liberally. The sentence of expulsion has frequently been carried out post-mortem."

"I am not my predecessors," Carlos said firmly. "You will return with us to the palace and be given quarters among my guards. Your movements will be circumscribed, but no other restraints will be placed upon you. You may eat and drink what you wish. A variety of women will be made available. These conditions will continue until you disclose the reason for your presence in Temalagua. After that you may do what you will. Leave. Stay. I have no intention of harming you. Should you decide to stay, well, I'm aware of your accomplishments—I'm certain you will have much to teach me, particularly as regards managing a business. And I'm equally certain that we will identify areas of common interest and have a great deal to discuss. You'll be a welcome addition to my court. Of course..." The king's smile seemed an article of complacent self-assurance. "You may choose to confess your motives here and now, and thus make all this unnecessary."

"What leads you to think that I would ever reveal my motives?" Rosacher asked.

Carlos' placid smile resurfaced. "We are much alike, Richard, you and I. In fact, I think we may be very nearly the same person. However, I have the advantage over you in that I have been this person since birth, while you have been forced, either by circumstance or some more powerful agency, to acquire the skills that have shaped our mutual character. Having this advantage, I know things that you do not, and one of these things is that eventually you will become bored with the unchallenging life I offer and will reveal your secrets if for no other reason than to create a dramatic episode."

Rosacher could not deny the truth of these words, but even as he admitted to Carlos' estimation of their kindred souls, it was as if he were receding from him, looking at him through the wrong end of a telescope, a view that enabled him to see that Carlos was, indeed, a well-intentioned man, a man capable, should he live, of doing great things, of changing the course of a nation and raising up an entire people from poverty; yet he would achieve this not because he was an altruist or a saint, but rather because he was a narcissist. Like all narcissists, like Rosacher himself, Carlos was likely prone to sudden shifts in temperament and, though by all reports the king had never varied from his benevolent pose, it *was* a pose. And thus it was possible that one day an event would transpire to turn him from a man whose ego was nourished by enacting good deeds to one with the capacity for unimaginable evil. Rosacher's impression of Carlos had been so thoroughly transformed, he felt at sea, inclined to let the night go forward without intervention, and he said querulously, "None of this would have occurred had you been more cautious in your foreign policy."

Carlos' smile faded, replaced by a wary look. "I don't follow. To what are you referring?"

"Your alliance with Mospiel," Rosacher said. "Your designs against Teocinte."

"Are you mad?" Carlos chuckled. "I have no designs against a country that is ready to tear itself apart. As for Mospiel, I'd sooner lie down with a *barba amarilla* than join with the prelates in any enterprise."

"Teocinte has never been so strong as now," said Rosacher.

"Perhaps I've been misinformed and your ties to the government in Teocinte are not as close as I imagined." Carlos splashed wine into his glass. "Could you be unaware of Breque's activities during the past year?" He sipped the wine and held the glass up so it caught the light; then he cast a sidelong glance at Rosacher. "Why have you come here?"

Rosacher ignored the question and said, "Councilman Breque has been a competent administrator. I haven't been diligent in my oversight for some months now—my interests lay elsewhere. But I trust Breque to do what's right for Teocinte."

"Then you placed your trust in a fool or a madman. Or both. Breque sends me letters reaffirming Teocinte's long-standing friendship with my country, and at the same time he has squandered a fortune on naval weaponry. Weaponry that can have no other purpose than an attack upon our ports. I might be concerned about this, but I have it on good authority that he has emptied his exchequer and has insufficient funds with which to buy ships. But you must know of this!"

Rosacher, shaken by Carlos' assertion, said, "How did you get your information? Are you certain it's accurate?"

"Oh, yes! In a short time, a few months, six months at best, Teocinte's economy will collapse. No matter how much mab is produced, your debts will come due well before you can expect to receive payment. They have already come due in many instances. Breque will have to sell his weaponry and reduce the price of mab in order to sustain even a feeble economy."

"The purchase of a few weapons...I can't see how that will topple the economy."

"Do you call seven hundred cannons a few? Six thousand rifles, the latest Russian model! One hundred armored war wagons designed to traverse the jungle, each large enough to carry a company! But you're right. These are only Breque's most recent expenditures, the ounce that tipped the scale. In the shipyards of Mataplan lie the keels of seventy great vessels that he has commissioned, intended to carry an invasion force...yet he cannot afford to complete them. I could recite a long list of Breque's ridiculous purchases. Apparently the man had designs on the entire littoral, perhaps the entire continent. But to whatever end, he has accumulated more weapons than he has soldiers, more ships than men to fill them. I have no fear of Teocinte. Your country is doomed. It's Mospiel I fear, for once Teocinte has been gutted by this idiot Breque, they will rush in and impose order, and there will be no buffer state between Mospiel and Temalagua." Carlos paused. "You have been duped, my friend. That much is clear from your reaction. But this raises the question, for what reason were you duped? And how does your presence here relate to that fact?"

A mosquito whined in Rosacher's ear. He slapped at it and, as if the slap were a cue, a grumbling noise issued from the jungle, then a roar that might have come from the throat of Griaule himself, so shattering it was—this followed by a volley of rifle fire and screams.

Carlos and Rosacher grabbed up their rifles, aiming them at the jungle. More screams, and Frederick, accompanied by a splintering of twigs and branches, burst from the shadowy foliage—Frederick as Rosacher had never before seen him, solidified into that bear-like shape that prior to this moment had only been hinted at, except in an artist's depiction. Standing on his hind legs, slashing at the air with taloned paws, roaring as rifles continued to fire, Frederick's torchlit reality was far more frightening than his portrait had been. In that posture he must have measured twenty feet from tip to toe, his body covered in coarse black fur, and as he swung his elongated head from side-to-side, its form that of a strange fruiting, some sort of mutant melon or squash, his face came into view, a leathery mask, slightly less black than the fur, that seemed to have been stamped onto the stump-end of a severed limb and had over time become a part of that limb, its nerves and musculature connecting, annealing with those of the stump, growing capable of gross movement, producing snarls and leers and various other expressions of rage and lust. His eyes were rheumy, redder than the artist had portrayed, and were set at more of a slant above the cheeks, giving him the aspect of a Tibetan devil god; but this was no brightly colored, ritualistic abstraction of evil, this was evil itself, evil incarnate, fanged and drooling and monstrous, with a lolling tongue and a furrowed brow and a quality of insane vacancy that somehow dominated the face, that was its base emotion.

All his thoughts of an alliance with the creature fled, scattered by fright, Rosacher fired, fired again, saw bullets strike home, eliciting an even greater roaring, dredging up gouts of blood from Frederick's cheek and forehead… then a shout from behind him: "Into the river!" A hand caught at his shoulder, yanked, and he pitched off the bank, landing on his back in the water. He went down beneath the surface and came back up sputtering, still holding his rifle, and sought purchase with his feet, but the river was too deep. He wiped the water from his eyes and saw Carlos' head an arm's length away. Four or five heads were visible farther upstream, but Rosacher could not identify them. Grumbling, Frederick—his body bulkier, more elephantine—prowled the water's margin and Rosacher thought that his lie about taking refuge in the river might have been intuitive and that they were safe. And then in the dimness, though he could not be sure of what he saw, the torches no longer flickering, the world drenched in shadow...he thought he saw Frederick lean out over the bank and extend his neck to an improbable degree, stretching to a length of four or five feet, bending to the river and snapping off one of the heads. Shouting in panic, the other swimmers flailed at the water. Rosacher let loose of his rifle, dove beneath the surface and swam as hard as he could for as long as he could without taking a breath. He came up for air and then dove again, repeating this process over and over until, exhausted, he fetched up against the far bank, tucking himself into a fold of shadow, an indentation in the clay, and clung there, alerted by every stirring and sound, however slight. At some point he passed out and when he awoke, his teeth chattering, he saw that a gray dawn had broken over the jungle. He hauled himself up onto the bank and stripped off his wet clothing. A gentle rain began to fall and, gathering his clothes into a bundle, he sought shelter beneath a giant silk-cotton tree, finding a dry spot amidst the roots that stretched out on all sides like the tails of caimans whose heads were trapped beneath the trunk. He stared blankly at the great gray-green dripping presence that pressed in around him, with its feathered fronds and nodding leaves the size of shovel heads that yielded a pattering like the drumming of childish fingers on the skin of a thousand small drums. The rain began to slant downward and its noise grew deafening; a chill settled in Rosacher's bones. He had no means of making fire and so he set forth walking, jogging when he found it possible...not often, because the trail he followed went uphill and down, often at sharp angles and with only a few yards between slopes. Rocks and roots jabbed at the soles of his bare feet, forcing him to a slower pace—he could not bear to put on his boots, because they reeked of the river and were packed with silt. He had not the least idea of his location or of the direction in which he was going. His thoughts congealed, his mind slowing as had his feet, and he became a sluggish machine capable only of lurching forward.

After a while, a very long while, it seemed, he smelled meat cooking. He crept along, uncertain whether he would find friend or foe, and shortly after that, he saw up ahead an embankment atop which an enormous tree had fallen, creating a natural shelter. Beneath it sat the king, shirtless, yet still wearing his riding trousers. Rosacher felt a measure of bitterness on seeing him so at ease. Relative to Rosacher, he was the picture of contentment—he had made a fire of branches and twigs, and was roasting the spitted carcass of a smallish animal. The prospect of warmth and food enticed Rosacher, but he hesitated to approach, mindful of how he would be received. Carlos carved a slice of meat from the animal's haunch with a skinning knife and laid it on some leaves to cool...and that was too much of a temptation for Rosacher. He started forward and, glancing up from the fire, Carlos said, "Richard! I thought you had drowned."

Rosacher dropped down beside the fire. His teeth still chattered and Carlos built the fire up, adding twigs and leaves until Rosacher's body had soaked up sufficient heat to allow him to think and speak. "What was that thing?" he asked, accepting a strip of meat that Carlos extended on his knife tip. The meat was greasy, but good.

"It's nothing I've seen before." Carlos sawed at the carcass. "I don't suppose you've encountered any other survivors."

Rosacher shook his head, No, and his teeth began to chatter again. Carlos urged him to rest and spread his clothes by the fire so they could dry.

Once his chill had passed, Rosacher had a second bite of the meat. "This is good. What is it?"

"Agouti." Carlos nibbled and chewed. "No one at court cares for the meat—they think it fit only for peasants. But I'm quite fond of it."

After Rosacher had finished his first piece of meat, the king carved him another. Rosacher had a bite and then, recalling why he had come to Temalagua, he asked Carlos if he knew what had happened to Cerruti.

"I can't be sure," Carlos said. "It was too dark to see clearly, but I think he was the one the beast decapitated."

His response started Rosacher to wondering why Cerruti had gone into the water. Had he been moved by instinct or had he been pushed? And if what Carlos told him was true, what did that say about the relationship between Cerruti and Frederick? His head was spinning and he was incapable of focusing on these questions, so he asked how Carlos had made his escape.

"I saw you go underwater and followed your example."

If Carlos said more, Rosacher was not aware of it, for he lapsed into unconsciousness. On waking, he discovered that the king had covered him with his doublet. He made to give back the garment, but Carlos refused to accept it, saying, "You're suffering from exposure. Don't worry about me. I'm fine."

The rain had been reduced to a drizzle and Rosacher's trousers were almost dry—he put them on and asked if Carlos knew where they were.

"About an hour east of Chisec, I believe. I haven't hunted this part of the jungle for years, but if memory serves, we follow this trail for about a half-hour and it intersects with something approximating a road. That should take us to the village." The king patted him on the shoulder. "Are you up to a little walk?"

"Give me a few minutes."

"We've plenty of time. It's not yet noon." Carlos added twigs to the fire. "I should be able to get word to the palace tonight. By tomorrow afternoon you'll be resting in comfort and I can get about organizing another hunt."

"You're going after that thing?"

"If there are no other survivors, I reckon it's killed more than twenty people. Allowing it to run free would be criminal."

"But how can you hope to destroy it?"

"If we can isolate it, hem it in against some natural barrier and trap it there, we may be able to set fires around the perimeter and burn it." Carlos spat into the fire. "I haven't given the subject much thought, but tomorrow I'll gather my huntsmen and we'll come up with a scheme. Something with alternatives in case things go awry."

However great a narcissist Carlos was, Rosacher thought, one couldn't fault his courage, though his judgment might be called into question. Once again he tried to put his commitment to the mission into perspective and once again he found himself testing the principles underlying its every facet—his concerns for the business, his quasi-loyalty to the disloyal Breque, and the idea that everything in his life had been a reaction to some fraudulent stimulus. When he first arrived in Teocinte, it seemed he'd had a plan, but he most certainly had not had one since then; he had been coerced and manipulated into every action, and now, understanding this, he wasn't able to assign a priority to any future action, least of all the murder of a king.

The rain kept the insects down—except for the leaf-cutter ants that carried bits of vegetation along the wire-thin tracks they had etched into the clay—and the two men spoke rarely during the first portion of their walk. Dark shapes in the canopy followed them for a time, but never announced their presence. The undergrowth thinned, the boles of silk-cotton trees became visible, like lotus columns inscribed with a calligraphy of livid green moss, and—in his fatigue—Rosacher imagined that they spelled out variations on his sorry fortune; he died in a green hell, his flesh was consumed by scorpions, beetles drank form the corners of his eyes, that sort of thing.

Carlos' estimate of a half-hour to reach the road to Chisec proved woefully inaccurate, too short by at least an hour; but reach it they did—a narrow winding track partially overgrown with weeds and displaying ruts caused by the passage of carts and wagons. Rosacher collapsed at the center of the road, his head dropping back, gazing up at the canopy. Carlos sat on a hump of clay covered by an ivy-like growth at the jungle's edge. "We've only a little ways to walk now. Twenty, twenty-five minutes."

"Your minutes seem considerably longer than mine," Rosacher said with bad grace.

Carlos kept silent, but his displeasure was obvious.

After an interval Rosacher, in lieu of an apology, said, "How can people live in this place?"

"The jungle? It's not so bad…in fact, it's fascinating. I love coming here."

"Spoken like a man with the wherewithal to protect himself from the worst it has to offer."

The king acknowledged this, making a noise of acquiescence. "You can protect yourself only to a degree. Witness last night. But you're right. The jungle's not a human place. People live here because it's where they were born. They don't have the motivation or the funds to move elsewhere. Still, it'll be a pity when it's all chopped down."

"I doubt that's going to happen."

"Admittedly the forests of western Europe are less pestilent than our jungles, yet when people needed room for expansion, they began to disappear. The same will happen here and then there'll be no more jungles, no more animals."

"I don't believe the countries of the littoral will ever achieve the level of economic stability that Europe has."

"That seems extremely shortsighted."

"The countries to the north of Temalagua have too great an advantage over you, both as to their size and resources. They've been waging a war of oppression for nearly a century. Look at how the fruit companies have moved in. They'll continue to oppress you until your leaders show some backbone or develop an immunity to bribes. Present company excepted, of course."

"Your argument strikes me as odd coming from someone who's spent decades propping up one such leader." Carlos scratched his calf vigorously. "But it's true. We have to have better leaders in order for our corruption to assume the guise of statesmanship."

Rosacher laughed. "You've got me there."

"One way or another, whether under our aegis or that of some other country, the jungles will soon be a memory. My father used to hunt jaguar in this very region and now you're lucky to catch sight of one."

"I'll consider myself lucky not to see one," said Rosacher.

"You might not say that if you'd seen what I have. A day's ride from here there's a lake to which my father used to take me. Lake Izabal. We'd find some high ground that overlooked the water, and hide in the tall grass before dawn, and wait for the jaguars to come down to drink while the morning mist still obscured most of the world. Watching a jaguar emerge from the mist—it gave me the feeling that I'd gone back to the days of creation."

Carlos leaned back, braced with both hands thrust into the dark green leaves. Rosacher was about to make an observation, a rather snide observation, when the king sat up straight and gave an exclamation of pain and shook his left hand—a banded snake no more than twenty inches long had sunk its fangs into the webbing between his thumb and forefinger, dangling there like a primitive ornament, striped red, yellow and black. Carlos' eyes locked onto Rosacher's. He appeared eager to speak, to communicate some desperate intelligence, but all that issued from his mouth was a throaty exhalation. Then he fell back, his face buried in the vegetation, the snake yet attached to his hand. The body underwent a series of tremors and lay still. And Rosacher, who had scrambled to his feet, looked on in confusion and shock as the snake retracted its fangs and slithered away among the leaves, disappearing with a flick of its tail that he found almost insouciant.

Knowing the king to be dead, Rosacher nonetheless searched for a pulse. Finding none, he felt suddenly imperiled. The jungle shrank around him, the air darkened, and the sounds, the scritches and chirrs, the buzz of flies, the chips and chirps from thousands of throats, many heralding the revolting feast that the king would soon become, signaling a troop of tiny nightmare creatures to gather at the banquet table...the horror of the natural world assailed him and he backed away, casting his eyes about so as to apprehend the next terror, the next sinister shape. To have survived the night and now this! Had his failure to assassinate Carlos caused the snake to enact Griaule's will? He forced himself to be calm and bent to the king. Turning the body, he removed the skinning knife from the sheath belted to his waist. Carlos' eyes showed all white beneath his drooping lids. Froth had collected at the corners of his mouth. Rosacher had the thought that he would be blamed for the king's demise. The idea was not entirely without justification. If he had not brought Frederick to Temalagua, the hunt would never have occurred... though he could scarcely be blamed for the snake, unless he was culpable on a cosmic level. He started to walk away and realized that Carlos had given no indication of which direction to take. He scanned the road in both directions, hoping to spot some clue or, barring that, to glean some intimation from the surround, some sense of human passage; but there was nothing other than the steady drip of the rain, the oppressive greenery, the phantasmagoric shapes made by the intersection of leaves, vines, stumps, mold and the shadows that defined them and the imagined beating of a predator's thirsty heart. The king's corpse seemed to have acquired a gravity that would not relax its grip, pulling at Rosacher. He covered Carlos' face with a handkerchief found in the doublet's pocket and the gravity dissolved. Since the king had been bitten on the left hand, he decided to go in that direction. He went a few steps, thinking how he should tell people what had happened—he had been on a hunt with Carlos, disaster struck and they had fled downstream, winding up near the road where Carlos had encountered the snake. But so much context was missing, it felt like a lie, and he supposed he felt that way because he had not been certain if his appreciation of the man was accurate. Carlos may have been a narcissist, yet perhaps his variety of narcissism was as close as humankind could aspire to producing a good man. He contemplated saying some words over the body, but couldn't think to whom he should commend the king's spirit, and so he set forth walking, heading for Chisec, for some fresh green hell, for whatever came next, focusing on the road ahead and trying not to let his mind linger over what might be following behind.

16

ROSACHER REMAINED IN TEMALAGUA for eight years. With more than a sufficiency of funds and cut loose from his responsibilities, he had no desire to return to his old life. He bought a house in a respectable quarter of Alta Miron and built up a business trading in exotic birds and animals, many of them sent to populate European zoos; but his chief preoccupation was with Frederick, who continued to terrorize the jungles east of the capital. The new king, yet another Carlos, possessed neither his father's altruism nor his concern for the security of his people, and had not the slightest interest in hunting down Frederick. Alta Miron was a fabulous city, offering diverse pleasures, but Rosacher rarely left his residence, motivated by Frederick's depredations to spend his days organizing hunts for the creature. He did not participate in these hunts; he had long since accepted the reality that he was not a courageous man. Sometimes, remembering Carlos, he doubted the existence of true courage, thinking that the king's bravery was the product of a misguided sense of invulnerability, and that the common strain of courage was a matter of venality; but he wasn't sure he believed this—the men he sent after Frederick had mastered their fears to an extent of which he was incapable and if courage was dependent on a profit motive, it was courage nevertheless. He paid the men well and made certain that they were conversant with the nature of the beast and the dangers involved. Some men were killed, but this failed to dissuade others from taking their place and, though they did not manage to kill Frederick, they succeeded over the years in harassing him, driving him south into the region known as the Fever Coast, a sparsely populated area, home mainly to smugglers and brigands—at this point, Rosacher decided that his responsibility was at an end and called off the hunts, leaving the human wreckage on the coast to fend for themselves and figuring that Frederick would go deeper into the jungle, away from the haunts of men, where animal life abounded.

News reached Rosacher from Teocinte. Makdessi's campaign against Mospiel had been successful, though Makdessi himself had not survived, and the rule of the prelates was no more. Many of them had been hanged in the square facing the palace. On hearing this, Rosacher thought of Arthur and how he would have loved to preside over the festivities. As for Teocinte's economy, Carlos' prediction did not pan out. The infusion of Mospiel's wealth into Teocinte's coffers staved off financial collapse and might have stabilized the economy, but Breque's continued expenditures kept the nation in a state of perpetual crisis, never able to catch up on their debts. Rosacher reacted to these reports with diminishing interest and it was not until eight years had passed, when the news that Griaule had wakened from his millennia-long slumbers and destroyed most of the city before giving up the ghost, thereby ending the production of mab...not until this came to his attention was he moved to visit the country he had once called home.

The establishment of a ferry between Temalagua and Port Chantay had cut the duration of the trip in half and, availing himself of this improvement in transportation, Rosacher arrived in Teocinte less than two weeks after the dragon's death. What he saw appalled him. The House of Griaule and, indeed, all of Morningshade, had been obliterated, either crushed beneath the dragon's body, which lay athwart the ruined city, or burnt to cinders by the fire he had vomited in his final assault on the world of men. Fire had destroyed the bulk of the city beyond Morningshade—the buildings atop Haver's Roost had survived, though not unscathed. The rear of the cathedral, now utilized as an orphanage, had been left in ruins and the government buildings had sustained minor damage. A vast tent city had sprung up among the charred ruins and there lived a population composed of survivors and émigrés, the latter mainly people who had come to scavenge the treasure hoard of Griaule's corpse. Cutthroats and pistoleros and scoundrels of every stamp ruled the place and you took your life in your hands by walking through its crooked byways. At every hour of the day and night, gunshots could be heard, bespeaking the minor wars fought between the embattled remnants of Teocinte's army, who strove to protect the rights of those who had made pre-mortem arrangements regarding the ownership of Griaule's scales, bones, organs, and so forth, and those who sought to possess these things extra-legally. Thousands of people swarmed over the carcass, hacking and slicing and prying. They had laid bare one of the dragon's ribs, the curve of bloodstained bone arching above the host of two-legged flies that milled beneath like the rib of an enormous unfinished ark, and gunfire also issued from dark crimson recesses of the body. Winches had been maneuvered into place and were engaged in removing the teeth and fangs. Men in butcher's aprons carted away huge slabs of meat. So many people were engaged in picking over the corpse, sawing at bones and scales, sampling fluids, even preying on the dragon's parasites, the gigantic worms that infested the dragon's bowels, Rosacher entertained the notion that he was observing the annihilation of a normal-sized lizard by a Lilliputian race of hominids who performed the functions of ants and beetles, and dwelled in a settlement of dirty gray canvas that hid the bulk of their repulsive habits from view. It was both an epic and dismaying sight, one that called to mind the majesty of nature and at the same time posed an inescapable comment on the vile nature of mankind. Rosacher was grateful that Griaule's flesh seemed to be rotting at a rate commensurate with the pace of his metabolic processes when alive—there was as yet only a hint of the stench that would saturate the atmosphere before too long.

On the morning following his arrival, Rosacher visited Breque in his home, a white-washed colonial-style mansion with a red tile roof, surrounded by palms and enclosed within high stone walls patrolled by armed guards. Due to its location behind Haver's Roost, the house and grounds had been shielded from destruction and appeared to exist in a tranquil country at a significant remove from the land on the dragon's side of the hill. A servant led Rosacher up a curving stair and along a corridor with mahogany panels carved into scenes of Teocinte's recent history—the fall of Mospiel, Breque's signature triumph, predominating—and at last into a gloomy, spacious bedroom where he found Breque's family gathered about a bed the size of a banquet table, canopied in green satin, where lay an unrecognizable shrunken personage whom he identified by process of deduction as Breque. A pale dust-hung shaft of light penetrated from a curtained window, painting a thin stripe up the center of the bed, and medicinal smells, particularly that of camphor, hung in the air. Word of the councilman's illness had been conveyed to Rosacher, but he had not expected this: Wisps of white hair floated above Breque's mottled scalp; his face was caved-in, blotched with liver spots, and his bony hands twitched atop the bedclothes like some kind of sea life that had been exposed by low tide and was being killed by the sun. Upon Breque's instruction, his wife, once a beauty, now reduced to a dry stick of a woman, ushered their two grown sons from the room and in a whispery voice Breque summoned Rosacher to come near. The reek of camphor was stronger close to the bed. Two dark, massive wardrobes hulked along the walls, looking in the shadows like silent, cowled witnesses.

"You haven't changed a bit, my friend." Breque's voice was stronger, as if enlivened by Rosacher's propinquity; but he drew a deep breath between sentences. "I marvel at your good health."

"I didn't realize you were so ill," said Rosacher.

"All life is an illness, whether of the flesh or of the spirit. I've grown accustomed to such frailties. This..." Breque's right hand made a palsied movement, a mere echo of what would have been a sweeping gesture in his prime. "Death is simply a shabby theatricality at life's end, one to which we all have been given tickets...with the possible exception of you."

It had been Rosacher's intention to seek redress for Breque's betrayal, but seeing him so debilitated, his resolve was blunted. "Oh, I'm not the man I was," he said. "I may not look my age, but I feel every year, believe me."

A chair stood against the wall and Rosacher pulled it around so that he could sit facing Breque. He was at a loss for something to say and he related the details of his meeting with Carlos and, given that Carlos' assertions were true, those concerning his lack of ambitions in Teocinte, he asked what Breque had hoped to gain by sending him on such an irrelevant mission.

"I wanted you out of the way when I attacked Mospiel. Your presence here might have had a deleterious effect in some way. If you succeeded in killing the king, I assumed the power of the Onyx Throne would be undermined, and that is never a bad thing. One of my many errors. This latest Carlos seems more likely to expand the borders of Temalagua than did his father."

The councilman's eyes seemed to have grown brighter as he spoke and he stared at Rosacher with a discomforting steadiness and avidity. Rosacher began to describe how he had spent the past eight years, but Breque interrupted him, saying, "I've kept my eye on you. As a matter of fact, I've purchased a number of birds from your company during that time…for my children's pleasure. And of course I've heard all about your efforts regarding Frederick. He's been chivvied down onto the Fever Coast, has he not?"

"According to reports, he has taken to hunting in the jungles across from Corn Island. A mangrove shore will prevent anyone from settling there and the jungle abounds with tapir and wild boar. I think we have heard the last of him."

"I should have liked to see him once."

"To see him as I did, that time on the Rio Coco...It is not a pleasant memory."

"Still..." said Breque, and fell silent.

Rosacher considered how to make a graceful exit—it seemed that he and Breque had little to tell each other, despite their long history together and, though Rosacher understood that his company pleased the councilman, he felt that if he prolonged his visit, things would become awkward. The minutes slipped away and Breque's ragged breathing became regular. Thinking him asleep, Rosacher made to stand, but Breque's arm shot out, his hand clutching Rosacher's wrist.

"Stay!" he said. "Just a little longer."

The sudden effort appeared to have sapped Breque's energies—his chest heaved, his breath wheezed, his eyes fixed on a spot in the satin canopy, and yet his grip on Rosacher's wrist grew no weaker. At length he turned his head, locking stares with Rosacher and, his voice straining with intensity, said, "We were great men!"

Rosacher did not know how he should respond, for Breque's words seemed at once a proclamation and a seeking of validation.

"You will deny it, I realize," Breque went on. "But we were great men. You moreso than I. I attempted great things and failed, but you achieved them."

"What did I achieve?" Rosacher asked. "Wealth? Many men achieve wealth and few of them are great."

"You killed Griaule! And in this, I was your accomplice. Together we destroyed a monster like none other the world has known."

"Cattanay killed the dragon."

"Cattanay was merely an instrument. It was your genius that enabled him, and it was mine to support you, to allow you to function. Yet I will be remembered only for my folly, and you may not be remembered at all. But we were..." His lips trembled. "We were...great men!"

His grip relaxed and then he let go of Rosacher's wrist.

"You won't accept what I've told you," said Breque in a faltering voice. "I know this. You've had to maintain a distance from people, an inhuman distance, in order to complete your work. The sole personal desire you have satisfied is your desire to be unhappy. The one woman you loved was one with a bleaker outlook on life than you. But hearing this from me may stop you from making too harsh a self-judgment. That is my hope for you."

Rosacher could not help being moved by these sentiments. His eyes watered and he wanted to offer a similar consolation to Breque, but he could not shape the words; they soured in his mouth and dissolved before he could speak them. The single comfort he could offer was to continue to sit with Breque, and this he did until the councilman asked for his family. Once they had entered the bedroom, Rosacher shut the door and sat down on a bench in the corridor to await the inevitable. His mind traveled back to the day he met Breque, waiting on a bench outside the council chamber, and he wondered briefly at this apparent circularity. He studied the carved mahogany panel across from him, warships approaching a coastal city, and realized that it was not a representation of the past, but depicted a future that would never occur—it had been commissioned in advance of Breque's planned invasion of Temalagua. The recognition increased his sadness and he thought of Breque's final message to him, not debating its truth or its purpose, but categorizing it, cataloguing it under the kindness of monsters, the charitable impulses of fiends, men responsible for thousands of deaths who at the end sought to bestow their blessing on the world.

He had been sitting in the corridor for fifteen or twenty minutes when he felt a wave ripple through his body and experienced a powerful shudder as of some vital passage. He went quietly to the bedroom door and cracked it, thinking that what he had felt was Breque's soul taking flight; but Breque's eldest son was bent over the councilman, his ear close to Breque's mouth, and it was clear that he was whispering some instruction or wish. Rosacher shut the door and sat back down. He could still feel the aftershocks of that passage, faint

tremors that came to him as might the inaudible rever-
berations of a gong, and he imagined that these heralded
the passage of a soul of much greater profundity than
Breque's, and that some crucial cut, some last insult to
the flesh, had loosed the dragon's soul from his decaying
body, freed him to fly out from his prison, casting a final
shadow over the city upon which he had waited so long
to avenge himself...or else it was a misperceived symptom of Rosacher's own decay, a minor unsteadiness of
the heart, a palpitation. From behind the bedroom door
there arose a muted wail. Rosacher stood and adjusted
the hang of his jacket. He was confident that he would
make the right noises, say the right things, for though
he found people unfathomable on an emotional level, in
a formal situation he could always be counted upon to
display appropriate behavior.

EPILOGUE

ON AN ISLAND FAR from anywhere Rosacher has built his home close to the shore. From the verandah he has an unimpeded view of the ocean, a cashew tree, and a strip of tawny sand criss-crossed by beachvine. If he leans forward and to the left, he can see the house of his immediate neighbor through a stand of palmettos—a little box set on stilts against the tides, painted light blue, a darker blue on the window frames. Beneath the house is a pen wherein pigs are kept. Once in a great while his neighbor, a black man named Peter, will shoot one of the pigs and butcher it. The remaining pigs appear to take no notice of the event. On Rosacher's right, the beach is lined with wind-bent palms and dotted with coconut litter—it stretches away toward a point of land, Punta Manabique, a place so pestilent that no one can dwell there. At night people walk along the shore, shining lanterns to light their way. Occasionally blood is shed over a woman or a property dispute, but otherwise it is a tranquil place, and it is this untroubled quality, this calm imperviousness to minor passions and upheavals that has encouraged Rosacher to put down roots here.

His mind often turns to Griaule—and how could it not?—and there are times when he suspects he may have witnessed the evolution of a god. Gods, he thinks, are produced by extreme circumstances and what could be more extreme than millennia of imprisonment, century upon century of striving to escape, learning to manipulate people and events to his benefit, growing ever more powerful, creating converts and eventually, having won his freedom, becoming discorporate, abandoning those people, and then, the final stage of evolution, going off somewhere to play a game of fiddlesticks, incomprehensible to all but himself. It's the kind of idea that once would have excited him, yet now induces boredom. Ideas in general no longer interest him, though he is rankled by the fact that his life seems to have no sum, no coherent shape, to be nothing more than a sequence of imperfectly realized scenes in an ill-conceived play.

For the longest time he feared that he would not die, that Griaule bestowed upon him an unwanted immortality; but now that he notices a stiffness in his limbs, an uncertainty in his step, a slight diminution of vision, all the minor failures of the flesh, he has come to feel at ease with himself as never before. All he needs of the world washes to his door. His neighbors' children scamper along the beach in front of Rosacher's house and he entertains them by playing the guitar, an instrument he took up when he first settled here, and by carving crude wooden toys. He is especially good at carving whistles. Women sail through his life, stopping for days, for a week, but he does not seek to hold onto them, he wants them to leave and, sensing this in him, they do. He has begun to dream of one woman in particular. She is quietly attractive, a slender brunette with a sly wit and a gentle manner. He pictures her in a white summer frock with an unobtrusive floral print. She teases him in his dreams, makes fun of his posturing, his foibles, but does so in a loving fashion. He is not the center of her world—she has her own obsessions and indulges them regularly, cultivating them with an artist's flair and a gardener's consistency. In bed she is fiercely concentrated, she assumes different shapes that conform to his, she takes as much as she gives, she promises him eternity without speaking a word. He thinks he will never meet her—she is someone he might have met had he not become involved with Griaule, if life had proceeded at a sedate rhythm, a Prussian waltz instead of a dervish whirl. And yet, knowing that the dream will have to suffice, he continues to look for her in every woman that happens along.

Of an evening, the people of the beach community come to sit on his verandah, singly for the most part, though on occasion a family will stop by, and they will talk of this and that, the weather, the fishing, their hopes for their children, a piece of gossip overhead in town. From time to time they will express their dissatisfaction with the direction of their lives, they complain about their lot and frequently express some need. They could use a new net, a communion dress for their youngest, a spirit level, a larger skiff, a more dependable clock, a cow to replace one that has died. Often, as if by a miracle, they will one morning find a communion dress neatly folded on their doorstep, a skiff bobbing at anchor just offshore, a net draped across the pilings of a rickety pier. Rosacher realizes that these small gifts are but another example of the kindness of monsters. He has no children and he is grateful that he did not have to watch a son grow to manhood, becoming in opposition to his father a person of sedate habits and accomplishments, viewing himself as a decent man, a moral entity, only to awake in the end to his own monstrous nature, his fundamental indifference to others' pain. The people of the beach have become his surrogate children, children he can keep at a distance and bless whenever the mood strikes. They appear to understand and respect the anonymity of his charity, infringing upon it only during moments of drunkenness during which they demand money or liquor or some other inessential that will do nothing apart from establishing a dependency—to these he does not respond.

Lately he has begun writing in a journal, recording fragmentary conversations, his observations of people and the natural world, bits of description and ironic commentary. A recent entry goes as follows:

✠

"Two weeks ago, while walking on the beach, I came upon a wooden whistle, one of mine, half-buried in the sand, carelessly tossed aside by a forgetful child. A tiny crab, no bigger than the nail of my little finger, had made its home inside it. Finding this conjunction of the crab and the whistle irresistible, appealing for its incongruity, I carried it home and set it on my verandah railing. The crab must have been terrified. It remained within the whistle for most of the evening, but I managed to entice it forth with a few crumbs of fish from my dinner plate. Having eaten, it scuttled merrily to and fro along the railing, seeming to have gained new confidence in its home, safe now from known predations and the erratic movements of the tides.

"I've fed it every night since and it appears to be growing larger. One day soon it will find the whistle too constraining and will emerge for a last time and explore fresh opportunities for food and housing in the wider world, or perhaps it will drift out on the tide, becoming for a brief span a mariner. I imagined it to be an exemplar among crabs, a crustacean genius nurtured by its musical house and taught to seek in all things a grand design, inspired to explore the possibility of land beyond Punta Manabique, to visit places that I, in my frail shell, cannot, sunset countries with beaches of rose and peach, surmounted by indigo cliffs and stars flashing signals from the depths of the universe that promise spectacular realms of light, infinite answers, a moral with which to caption our petty tale...but then my reverie was interrupted by Walker James joining me on the stoop, and the thought of answers and morals evaporated as he chatted about his day, discussing his daughter's earache, the girth of his prize sow, and the cupidity of a local tavern owner, a man who 'wouldn't stand you a drink unless the sun duppy come down and sour his whiskey.' On an island of storytellers, he was acknowledged one of the best, and that night he told how the tavern owner became infatuated with a Spanish lady from the mainland and the increasingly ludicrous acts he performed in his efforts to win her affections. Thereafter we sat for a while, enjoying the heavy crush of the surf and the palm fronds lashing in a north wind that threatened a storm by morning, the sky beyond Manabique ablaze with a shrapnel of golden fire. Then Walker heard his name called by a woman's voice from off along the shore. He stood and stretched, working out a crick in his spine, his head thrown back.

LUCIUS SHEPARD

"'Look at all that glory. Richard,' he said, gesturing at the heavens. 'Don't it make it make you a trifle sad sometimes, how we won't never hear a story to match all this sky and stars?'"